W9-CKI-748

THE DARK AND BLOODY GROUND

Stories of the American Frontier

THE
DARK

AND BLOODY GROUND

STORIES OF THE AMERICAN FRONTIER

selected by

PHYLLIS R. FENNER

illustrated by Charles Geer

WILLIAM MORROW & CO. • NEW YORK • 1963

This book is for
Nancy,
a pioneer woman—sort of.

CONTENTS

A WORLD OF FRONTIERS

I have heard it asked, "Will we be able to stand the strain of living in a world of uncertainty, of cold wars, and of atom bombs, today, tomorrow, and perhaps even the day after tomorrow?" The answer is to be found in the past. For many generations our people lived in a world of frontiers with its struggles, dangers, and hardships. Men cultivated their fields with muskets by their side. Women stayed alone in pioneer cabins and sod huts with weapons handy, ready to use them. Children grew up with the feeling of danger ever present. These men and women gave up backgrounds of culture, comfort, and security to face the wilderness, a dark and bloody ground, for the sake of an ideal of freedom or love of the land, and some in search of adventure.

P.F.

THE DARK AND BLOODY GROUND

Stories of the American Frontier

END OF THE TRAIL

JIM KJELGAARD

They lay together by the trail—a broken axle, a dead ox, and an elaborately carved chest of drawers filled with household goods. Jim Clyman swung off his horse to examine them. The little brown dog that had been running beside him edged curiously up to sniff at the ox, and the horse blew through its nostrils. Jim Clyman reached up with his left hand to scratch the gray stubble on his chin. He looked westward, where the ominous spears that were the peaks of the Sierra Nevada Mountains arched endlessly to reach the sky, and studied the nest of clouds that were gathering over them. A broken axle, a dead ox, and a chest of drawers. . . . The little brown dog wagged his tail at him, and Jim Clyman spoke as he would have to a man.

"There's gonna be trouble ahead, Bub."

The brown spaniel reared with both front paws against his master's thigh, and shoved his nose into the cupped hand. The old mountain man stroked the dog's ears absently, and spat into the rutted trail. There was going to be trouble, sure enough, although not this time from the Indians. The Arikaras, Arapahos, and Blackfeet had been tamed back in the early twenties, when the mountain men and the trappers had been the only ones to hit the trails west of the Missouri. Tenderfeet now traveled those paths which the feet—and the blood—of the mountain men had marked. Now tenderfeet needn't fear the Indians—anyhow, not very much. But they didn't take into proper account the much more savage enemies of mountains and distance and weather with which they had to cope in this year of 1844, when every tenderfoot, all his brothers and sisters, sons and daughters, uncles, aunts, and grandparents seemed to be either on the way to California or Oregon, or obsessed with the idea that they must soon start.

A broken axle, a dead ox, and a chest of drawers filled with household goods. . . .

Jim Clyman spat again into the rut, and did some thinking. There had been six wagons in this party ahead of him when he left Fort Bridger, back in Wyoming. Their trail had freshened considerably just after he left the Humboldt Sink. Now five of them had gone on, and might already be over the divide above Truckee Lake. The sixth had broken down; its occupants had taken time out to make another axle, and the cow that had been tied to the back of the wagon had been yoked in to take the dead ox's place. The team that now pulled this wagon was a very tired one. Women, Jim Clyman reflected, would hang on to their household goods until the last gasp. They'd keep the chest unless it just had to be thrown out so the wagon could be lightened and half-dead cattle could still stagger on toward the land of promise, the milk-and-honey land of California.

The old mountain man looped the horse's reins over his arm and started to walk along the trail, his eyes on the ground. Trotting placidly beside him, the little brown dog waved his tail and gave all his attention to snuffling through the rut in which he walked.

The long trail to the promised land, Jim Clyman thought, was surely marked with heartache. The path taken by these people was strewn with dead oxen, and graves, and broken wagons, and chests, and tools, clear back to the old homes from which they had come. Why did they get themselves a yoke of oxen, or a team of mules and a covered wagon, cast everything else aside, and hit the long stretch clear to the West? Jim Clyman answered his own question aloud.

"I know why, Bub," he said to the dog.

Back in New England homesteads, while battling their way through drifts to feed cattle, men thought of perpetually green fields where cattle could graze all winter. Or, while guiding a plow through stubborn, rock-strewn earth, they dreamed of soft black soil where plows never bucked. Or women in storm-lashed prairie huts conjured up images of flowers blooming at Christmas, or zephyr-soft breezes instead of blizzards. The West was a rich and sunny land where every woman was a queen and every man a king. It was thus that these people had talked to themselves and, talking, convinced themselves that they should go to Oregon or California. But they were deluding themselves and they knew it. Deep in their hearts they were aware that they had to go West for the same reason that Columbus had to sail for America. All about was sameness, and unchanging ideas, and routine, and satisfied people who were content to cope with the world they knew. But if there was something new to discover, an opportunity to be seized, a challenge to be met, *they* wanted to do it.

"That's the answer, Bub," Jim Clyman said.

He sighed and mounted his horse. People who blindly obeyed a beckoning finger that bent in their direction were always getting into messes, and this was going to be a bad one if somebody didn't come along to get them out. There were two men, a woman, and two children with the wagon ahead, and they were walking. He had found out that much while he studied their trail. Again he looked at the piled masses of clouds over the mountains, and shook his head.

It was a long, cruel trail that the immigrants had followed. Along it many a man, woman, and child, bereft of their own horses or wagons, had been refused permission to use someone else's. They had had to walk, and it was a singular thing that they had nearly always walked toward the magic lodestone that drew them to the West. They had walked until they died—except for those very few who had walked clear to California. But all the luck in the world had been on the side of those who had finally made it.

And the cruelest part of the entire trail was the divide above Truckee Lake. It was only a year ago that Jim Clyman had helped another train of six wagons get over it. They had hitched four span of oxen to a single wagon, and they had strained up the slope until some of them had died from the terrific strain. Other oxen had been brought to replace the dead ones, and behind the wagon men and women had pushed. But that had been a train with oxen to spare, and no snow had yet fallen on the slopes.

Jim Clyman spurred his horse, and the animal broke into a little trot. His old friend, Caleb Greenwood, had been guiding that other train. Most of the mountain men, now that it was no longer profitable to trap beaver, guided immigrants on the California or Oregon Trail. Caleb had been seventy-nine last year, but after they had finally come down from the mountains he had taken his gun and gone back up to get himself a mess of bear meat. The mush-and-milk food of the wagons, he had said, had run him down seriously. Jim Clyman smiled in recollection.

A day and a half later he rode his horse into Truckee Meadows and saw what he had known he would see there.

A fifteen-year-old boy, dressed in homespun and carrying a rifle, turned to stand beside the trail when he heard the horse. The little brown spaniel padded forward to meet him, and the boy stretched out a hand to stroke the dog's ears. The mountain man reined in his horse and dismounted.

"Howdy, Son. My name's Jim Clyman."

The boy tossed back his head, to fling the long, straight hair out of his eyes, and continued to tickle the dog's ears. "I'm Nathan Parker," he said. "I'm afraid you're in a bad way, Mr. Clyman."

"So?"

"You can't get over the divide. We tried it. We drove the three oxen and a cow up ahead of us to break a path.

But the snow's too deep to go on. We stayed on the slope all night, and it snowed. The next morning we couldn't go on at all. We had to come back down and build a camp to spend the winter in."

"What happened to the oxen and cow?"

"We got the cow back down—she hadn't been hitched for a long pull. But the oxen died right there in the snow and are all covered up now."

Jim Clyman writhed inwardly. You could always trust a tenderfoot to get himself into trouble, and then to make it worse with his own foolishness. A mountain man, knowing the divide to be snowed under, never would have taken the oxen up in the first place. A party aiming to winter had to have food, and the weather-wise game had already gone from these heights. Three oxen would have lasted five people for a long time. But they were gone, and there was only the cow left.

"Got any grub in your wagon, Nate?" he asked.

"Not very much." The boy flushed with pleasure. A man, evidently one who understood this country, had called him Nate and was asking him questions. "All we got is just a little flour and beans, and Mr. Cressman's got those."

"Who's Mr. Cressman?"

"The man travelin' with us. It was really his flour. He owns the cow, too."

"Looks like Mr. Cressman aims to have vittles for a spell," Jim Clyman muttered. "Who else is along?"

"My Uncle George and Aunt Kate—their name's Parker, too. Uncle George is out huntin'. Then there's my little cousin, Ann. She's almost four. Are you goin' to stay with us?"

"I dunno just what's to be done, Sonny. S'pose we toss a stick in the air and see how she lands. I got a few blocks of pemmican in my saddlebags, and it looks like we're goin' to need 'em."

They walked together up the trail, the little brown dog frisking ahead of them. A cold blast of air surged down from the top of the mountains. A few scattered flakes of snow trailed on the wings of the wind, and the angry brood of clouds glowered at them. Jim Clyman smelled wood smoke, and a moment later they came within sight of a broken-down wagon and two brush tepees built at the base of a huge pine. Beside one of the shelters hung the freshly butchered carcass of a cow.

"I'll bet that'll be Cressman's dugout," Clyman grunted.

"Yep. He won't—"

Nate was interrupted by a woman who came out of the other side. She was tall, with clear blue eyes that were set far apart. The little girl who clung to her skirt was a tiny image of her mother. Jim Clyman nodded respectfully.

"Howdy, ma'am."

"Oh—hello. I had hardly expected—"

Nathan Parker said, "It's Mr. Jim Clyman, Aunt Kate. I found him riding up the trail. Uncle George get anything to eat?"

"He's not back yet." The woman looked questioningly at him, then down at the little girl. She hesitated.

Jim Clyman understood. On the road to California you were always welcome at any camp—so long as there was plenty of food in it. He reached into his saddlebag, got one of the pemmican blocks, and cut it in two with his knife. Half of it, and the three remaining blocks, he slipped into the spacious pocket of his jacket. The little dog looked up pleadingly, but his owner looked away from him, at the woman.

"I'm right glad to know you, ma'am. Here. There's a lot of git in pemmican. Why don't you sort of cook up a meal for the little girl and yourself?"

The woman looked down again, and when she raised her head, tears brimmed in her eyes. Clyman looked away, pretending not to hear the thanks that she called after him, and walked over to the tree where the butchered cow hung. As he reached up his knife for a piece of the meat, a warning voice came from the other shelter.

"Leave it alone."

The little dog backed against his legs, growling, and Jim Clyman stopped, knife in hand, to look at the stocky, dark-haired man who emerged from the other shelter.

"I'll bet you're Cressman."

"I'm Cressman, and that's my beef. Leave it alone."

Without seeming to move fast, the mountain man took three steps forward and dug the point of the knife into Cressman's pudgy stomach. His voice was mild but steady.

"It's camp meat and I'm takin' charge of it. I'm takin' the flour, too."

"You are not!"

"If you want to argue the point, we'll fight it out here and now, and see who's gonna be boss."

Cressman muttered belligerently, but without looking at him again Jim Clyman cut off a piece of the beef, walked past the other into the brush shelter, and picked up the small keg with the few pounds of flour in it. Nathan Parker padded beside him as he strode away.

"He'll be mad at you!" he said in an awed voice.

"Well doggone, I've went and made somebody mad! Take this meat and flour in to your Aunt Kate. The flour's for whoever needs it most, and I'm sayin' who needs it. Tell her to have a good hot stew ready for your uncle when he comes back."

The boy disappeared in the shelter, and Clyman unsaddled his horse. He rubbed the animal's nose a moment, then stood back and shot it through the head. An almost inaudible sigh escaped him. It had been a good horse, a faithful and intelligent horse. But when people's lives were in the balance a horse didn't count.

He sighed again. Of all the dang fools ever created, a mountain man was probably the dangdest. He and the horse and the dog could have gone over the divide. But only the most abysmal fool would think of coming into a camp of stranded immigrants, taking charge of it, and trying to take them over, too.

He had butchered the horse and was hanging it up, when he saw a man emerge from the pine trees and walk through the steadily falling snow. Except for his rifle, he was empty-handed. Clyman pretended not to see, until a voice spoke from behind him.

"Hello, stranger."

"Why, howdy," Clyman said, turning as if in surprise. "You must be George Parker."

"That's right."

He was a thin man with pale blond hair and a hesitant manner. The mountain man's heart sank. It was certainly going to be a mismated crew that left this camp to go over the divide. Kate and George Parker, two sensitive, high-strung people with a fine native courage but no experience. Cressman, a selfish man ready to turn beast whenever that was expedient. A little girl who, at the best, would be an encumbrance, and a fifteen-year-old boy. He looked again at the blond man. George Parker seemed as though he'd be all right so long as he didn't have to face any difficult decisions, and then make them himself.

"Say, George," he said, "bring your wife, Nate, Cressman, and the little girl out here, will you? We got to have a powwow."

He stood near the place where he had butchered the horse, and the little brown dog came up to nuzzle his hand. He waited until the stranded wagoners were gathered about him, then addressed himself to George Parker. "How'd the huntin' go, George?"

Parker flushed. "I guess I'm not very good. I couldn't even see any game."

The mountain man shook his head grimly. "There ain't any to see; it's all gone down inta the valleys, where food's easier to get. So we'd starve to death if we tried to winter here. We got to go over the divide."

For a moment there was silence, as each in turn pondered this information.

"What assurance is there that we can do it?" Kate Parker asked.

"None. None a tall. The only sure thing is we'll starve if we don't do it."

He saw that pronouncement hit home with all the impact of a bullet. These tenderfeet wanted to go to California, not to starve. And they'd follow anybody who talked as though he were able to take them there, even though they had never seen him before today.

"I'm ready," Cressman growled.

"Well," George Parker said, looking at his wife, "well, I guess we'd better try."

"It looks," Clyman said deliberately, "like there ain't a vote ag'in it. We got more meat here than we can carry, and I want everybody to eat's much as they can before we start. Even if you got to stuff it down, do that. Mrs. Parker, save most of the flour for the little girl. George, I'll want your wagon spokes."

"What for?"

"For snowshoes. Spokes are good frames, and I'll lace 'em with hide. You and Cressman get in all the wood you can and take a big passel of meat inta the shelters. This snow's gonna fall hard, and we can't start till it's over."

It snowed hard for eight days—at first soft, feathery flakes, and then hard, crystalline ones that piled on top of the shelters and dribbled through the cracks in them until more snow added itself to that already there and stopped up the cracks. It piled up on the pine branches until they became overloaded and spilled their burdens. Driven by the wind, it formed long, curling drifts against every obstruction. And, when the storm finally passed, threatening clouds still hung over the divide.

During those eight days Jim Clyman, Nate, and the two Parkers had worked shaping the wheel spokes into snowshoe frames, scraping the hair from the horsehide and cowhide, slicing them into thin strips, drying these before the fire, and lacing the dried strips across the frames. Snow was piled high about the shelter, but the fire lit the interior, and sent its blue smoke climbing up through the smoke hole in the roof, which was kept open by poking a long stick up through it. The kettle bubbled constantly, melting snow for drinking water and simmering endless stews. Mealtime was any time anyone felt like eating. They could afford to be prodigal with their food when they could not possibly carry all of it with them, and every ounce they ate now added to their strength.

On the morning of the ninth day, probing through the smoke hole with his stick and finding no snow to push away, Jim Clyman took the shovel that he had brought in from the wagon, and began to dig. The snow, eight feet of which had fallen in eight days, was almost even with the top of the rude shelter. Working the point of his shovel up along the side of the door, he pushed the snow aside, and blinked in the unaccustomed flood of light. He continued to dig, enlarging the hole. Then, cutting steps as he went, he dug upward and outward, and emerged into a white, silent world. To one side, the shelter in which Cressman had crouched alone for eight days was only a soft mound on top of the snow blanket.

Jim Clyman slipped his feet into the harnesses of the homemade snowshoes and walked over to Cressman's shelter. He shoveled a hole down to the door, shouted, and when muffled sounds emerged, dropped the shovel down. Cressman had survived, and could dig himself out.

Young Nate Parker, who had come out of the shelter to try his first experimental steps on snowshoes, floundered over. "Say, is this snow deep!" he panted.

The little brown dog frisked happily about, his big paws better support on the crystalline crust than the snowshoes of the heavier human beings. The mountain man watched thoughtfully, his lips pursed. A dog was really something to have when a man was out this way. The least you could say about him was that he never worried. But then, neither did young 'uns—all Nate Parker could think about was the wonderful depth of the snow. But he could take care of himself. Ann couldn't, and it was going to be a mite of a problem to get the little tyke over the divide and down the other slope.

He reached over to slash the thong that bore a twenty-pound chunk of horse meat aloft on a pine branch, and caught it in his hands as it fell.

"Take this inside, will you, Nate?" he called.

The boy carried the frozen chunk of meat into the tepee, and a moment later his uncle and aunt came out. They glanced at the shelter where Cressman had cleared a hole for himself and was working to shovel his way to the top of the snow, then set to work helping carry the rest of the meat into their shelter. With the ax, Clyman began chopping the frozen stuff into thin slices, then used his knife to pare the rest of it from the bones. He had begun to make up four packs when Cressman came down into the shelter and stood sullenly watching him.

"Where's the fifth one?" Cressman demanded.

Jim Clyman said reasonably, "I figger we men can pack mebbe thirty-five pounds each up the slope. Nate's takin' twenty-five."

"What about her?"

"The little girl can't wear snowshoes, so somebody's got to help her all the time, and carry her some of the time. We'll take turns."

Cressman sputtered belligerently. "You know we ain't got much chance of gettin' out of here unless we haul every ounce of food we can!"

"We're takin' four packs." Clyman's voice was smooth. "I told you before I'm big buck at this lick."

Cressman subsided, and Jim Clyman went on making up the packs. He folded a portion of the meat in a square torn from the wagon cover, and formed broad shoulder straps with more of the same material. A blanket was tied to each pack, and two to his own. The little remaining flour he wrapped in a strip of buckskin and put in his own pack. Finally he hung his powder horn at his belt and put half a dozen bullets in his pocket. One rifle was enough. More would be extra weight. He rose.

"Cressman, you carry the ax."

"I'll carry it," Nate Parker offered.

"Cressman will."

He climbed up the steps he had chopped and stood for a moment in the snow on top of them. The little dog crowded close to his heels and squatted down on the tails of his snowshoes while he waited for the rest to join him. They started west toward the slope, Kate Parker and Ann behind Clyman, then Cressman, with George and Nate Parker bringing up the rear. Jim Clyman walked a quarter of a mile and turned around. Kate Parker smiled at him. But there was sweat on her face and she was breathing heavily.

The mountain man went on without slowing his pace. It was a right long way over the pass and down the opposite slope, and they'd better push it hard while they were well-fed and rested. When, and if, they got out of these mountains, they might be crawling on their hands and knees. He studied the clouds that hung low over the mountain peaks, and pushed on another mile before stopping. Then he waited for Kate Parker to close the gap that had imperceptibly widened between them. She was now carrying Ann.

"That little mite you got there," he said, "could rest easy as nothin' on top of my own pack for a spell."

"I'll carry her, Mr. Clyman," the mother said with quiet dignity.

Clyman turned and went on. Immigrants bound for California might be senseless folks who hadn't the least idea of how to take care of themselves. But there was no denying that some of them possessed courage of a sort to brighten the eye of the doughtiest mountain man. Kate Parker's baby was going over the divide with her. She might have to pant to hold up her end. But her baby was still going with her.

The next day they struck the steepest part of the slope and began to claw and fight their way up it. Storm clouds milled angrily above them, and it was bitingly cold. Jim Clyman stopped to turn and look back through the half-gloom, and his brown dog gladly sat down in the tracks he had made. One by one the rest struggled up and stood panting near him. The mountain man measured with his eye the distance to the top of the divide, and anxiously studied the clouds. A rising gust of wind blew a whirling line of snow around them. Not seeming to hurry, but still moving purposefully, Jim Clyman paused behind each pack-laden man and cut the blanket from his back. He spread two of them on the snow.

"We ain't goin' to make it," he said in a matter-of-fact voice. "Sit in a circle on these blankets, and I'll put the others over us. Every person's responsible for holdin' down his part. The baby goes in the middle. We ain't gonna freeze if we do it right. It's an old mountain man's trick."

They sat down on the blankets obediently enough. Clyman pulled the rest over them, tucking them in closely. He

closed the last gap with his own body as the storm began
to rage down in full fury. Dry snow piled on top of the im-
provised tent. The little dog whimpered in the darkness, and
the child talked baby gibberish. All that night, nibbling at
the pemmican that they carried, they crouched under the
blankets and kept each other warm with body heat. Then
they pushed the snow from the blankets and, rising like
specters, floundered on their way through the soft snow.

That day they got over the divide. Jim Clyman stood at
the top of it, waiting for the rest to straggle up. First Cressman came. Then Nathan Parker appeared and, finally,
George and Kate Parker, the father carrying Ann. The
mountain man stared at them silently. Coming up that mur-
derous, snow-filled slope, George Parker had thrown his
food pack away to help his wife and baby. Jim Clyman
could not find the heart to reproach him. He turned to start
down the slope.

"I was wrong about him, Bub," he muttered to the tired
little dog. "He *can* make up his own mind."

Two days later Jim Clyman turned off the trail into the
forest. With the ax that he had taken from Cressman he
chopped down four small trees. He trimmed the branches
from them, and cut the trunks in half. Then he arranged
the logs on the ten feet of snow that lay there, made a little
pile of shaven pitch-pine sticks, and poured a pinch of
powder from his powder horn. He struck a spark into the
powder, and the fire flared up. The little brown dog lay
near the comforting warmth, paws outspread and tongue
lolling expectantly as he glanced up at his master.

The mountain man looked back up the irregular line of
snowshoe tracks he had made coming down, and frowned.

He and the dog could have been another fifteen miles down the slope by this time. But you couldn't travel that way with tenderfeet. Not that anyone except Cressman had hung back, or complained of the cold and hunger. They just weren't making it so well. George Parker and his wife were taking turns carrying the little girl, but they had to rest every little while. Nate, the boy, had plodded steadily along with his lightening pack—and it had been lightened because Jim Clyman insisted on using the food he carried before any other. Now that was gone, and Parker's was gone. He would start using Cressman's tonight, and save his own for the last hard stretch. He had rationed the food carefully, and they should make it if the tenderfeet could keep up and if another bad blizzard didn't hit them.

As he threw more wood on the fire, the dog rose from his bed in the snow and cocked his head up the trail. Nathan Parker appeared, stumbling down the snowshoe tracks with his head bent and his eyes streaming. The sun had shone brightly all day, and the Parkers and Cressman couldn't seem to get the knack of avoiding snow blindness by squinting properly. But there was no point in exaggerating burdens, or stressing them.

"Doggonit, Nate," he said, "I thought you'd took off on another track."

"Nope." The boy gave a tired grin and sat down to slip the blanket from his shoulders. "I'll stick."

"Reckon you will. Well, fire's ready. Where's the others?"

"They're comin'."

Kate and George Parker, with the little girl riding on her father's shoulders, staggered along the trail and threw themselves wearily down by the leaping fire. Tired as she was, the mother took the child and cradled her in her arms.

Jim Clyman petted his dog, and watched them reflectively. Once a mountain man had come stumbling into his camp. He had traveled almost seven hundred miles through hostile country, he said, and for the past nine days he had had nothing to eat. Many times he had been tempted to give up and die, but he had kept himself alive by thinking of the buffalo steak he was going to have as soon as he got into somebody's camp. That man had lived on hope. Hope was a wonderful thing, a sustaining resource when all others failed. The Parkers had it in large measure.

Cressman came in to the fire and sat with his head hunched over his chest, staring with vacant eyes at the flames. Clyman looked keenly at him. Cressman, the laggard, who had been hanging back more than anyone else the past three days, seemed more fit and ready to go on than any of the others. His face fuller; his color better. But his expression was becoming more beast than human. The old man's eyes narrowed.

"Let's have your pack, Cressman. Time for grub—such as it is."

"My pack? *My* pack . . . ?"

Cressman raised his head, and glanced crookedly about. He dropped the pack, and the mountain man stepped forward to unfasten the thongs that bound it. But even before he did he knew that it was empty. He took a step forward, his knife in his hand. A deep anger leaped within him, and red shapes wavered before his eyes.

"You ate it!" he snarled. "You ate it, didn't you? That's why you hung back!"

The hot cloud of rage slowly dissolved, and he again became the leader of the little group. Dimly he saw the rest looking at Cressman, saw civilized eyes glowing red in the reflection of the fire, betraying a deep, elemental passion that went far, far back. They were primitive people, cave people who had seen their food stolen. Cressman did not notice them. His eyes were rolling, a vacuous grin played about his lips. The trail was driving him mad.

"Eat the dog," he babbled. "We c'n eat the dog."

Jim Clyman stuck his knife in a log, drew his pack to him, and pulled out a small piece of frozen meat. He saw the eager eyes of the Parkers fixed upon him now, the greedy eyes of the half-mad Cressman. Cressman started to rise, his hands twitching. Clyman reached for his knife.

"Sit down!" he growled. "Mebbe you eat tomorrow, but not tonight. You've had your'n!"

He cut two thin slices of meat for each of the others, impaled them on sticks, and put them over the fire to cook. Melting snow in the kettle, he stirred a little flour into it, flavored it with a tiny piece of meat, and handed it to Kate Parker. The baby ate hungrily, but when the mother was given her own ration, she shook her head.

"Can't I save it for tomorrow?"

Beneath her question was a deeper and more penetrating one. There was tomorrow, and the next day, and the next. . . . The baby had to eat all those days. The future generation must survive.

"Eat it now," Jim Clyman said gruffly.

She did, tearing the meat into tiny morsels with her teeth and devouring them reluctantly. While they ate, Clyman never took his eyes from Cressman. But the man was apathetic, mumbling to himself and smiling foolishly. When they had finished, the mountain man spoke as cheerfully as he could.

"I been in such fixes before, and I'll be in 'em ag'in. We're

gonna get through. But if anybody touches my pack, I'll
kill him."

"Eat the dog," Cressman raved. "Kill and eat the dog."

Clyman glanced across the fire at him, and said nothing.
But when he rolled up in his blanket that night, the dog
was beside him.

Jim Clyman himself was not exactly sure as to what took
place the next few days. He knew only that the two slices
of meat were cut to one, and that when they finally came
out of the deep snow they cut the lacings from their snowshoes, boiled them, and drank the gelatinous soup. The
last of the meat he carried had been eaten yesterday morning, while starved eyes had looked at the little brown dog
and then guiltily away again. This morning the baby had
had the last of the flour.

He walked on, the spaniel dragging wearily at his heels.
On either side the tall pines rustled, and the racing little
brook he was following cast itself furiously over the ice-
sheathed rocks and boulders in its path. It seemed that he
was back at the time when the starved hunter had wandered into camp. That memory was very plain and very
sharp. The hunter, he remembered, had lived entirely on
hope, on the hope of a meal of buffalo meat. But tenderfeet
weren't mountain men. They wouldn't believe that they
were going to get anything unless they could see it before
them. And all they could see was his dog. . . .

He forced himself back to reality. Behind him were people, hungry people, each of whom, in his own way, thought
of the things nearest and dearest to him. Cressman, in his
insane wanderings, had gone back to his farm on the Fox
River and was enjoying all the things it had once offered

him. Nathan Parker thought of going on, of continuing to follow this man who had dared suggest coming over the divide when it was impassable. George and Kate Parker thought of the child in her arms, and of all the life that was to be.

But their whole minds, when they were at either the morning or the evening fire, centered on the little brown dog and the salvation he offered. Here was food, and food was life, and they had to live. They could not be lured this far, then die within reach of their goal. He turned aside and gathered wood for a fire. He poured a little gunpowder under the wood and lighted it. Tonight they would camp out of the winter snow. The little dog lay down before the fire with his head on his paws.

Nathan Parker appeared, and almost as soon as he sat down beside the fire his eyes fastened on the dog. Carrying the little girl between them, Kate and George Parker came stumbling out of the semi-gloom. Cressman crawled up, babbling of fat sheep that had grazed beside the Fox River and of the many meals he had eaten there. Then he, too, fell silent, and all eyes were fixed on the dog.

Jim Clyman edged his knife out of its sheath. An animal was not supposed to mean anything when human lives were at stake, but the little spaniel was more to him than any person. He was a friend, one to whom he could confide his innermost thoughts and troubles, one who had always been satisfied to share his fortune. The knife point stopped at the dog's throat, and Clyman held it there while he looked at the eager people about the fire. They had been led on by tangible hope, by the certain knowledge that, when their last food gave out, they had a final resource in the dog. And they could go no farther without food. The

dog would feed them tonight, tomorrow, and perhaps the
day after. It would see them through. He touched the knife
against the dog's throat, and the spaniel whimpered in his
arms.

"Well, by God!"

It was not a curse but a prayer, and it came from outside
the circle of firelight. A tall man with a rifle in his hands
stood there, a strong, well-fed man with a pack on his back.

"You came over the divide?" he asked incredulously.

They struggled to their feet, staring in disbelief at this
man who had brought them salvation. The caveman had
gone from them. They were once again civilized, thinking
people.

"Got caught out on a long survey," the stranger explained, "and saw your fire. Our camp's only a piece down
the trail, but I reckon you'd better eat right here." He
swung his pack to the ground.

Jim Clyman slowly slipped his knife back in its sheath,
and tickled the little dog's ears with a bony finger. "We
made it, Bub," he said huskily. "We made it. This here's
the end of the trail."

NOT TOO HARD

HOWARD FAST

All in the cabin had a sense of being imprisoned, even the four-month-old baby, who lay on her back and whimpered for her mother's milk. It was hot in the cabin—midsummer heat—and six persons filled it to overflowing. It wasn't a very large cabin.

The boy was eight years old, tall for his age and skinny; he had a round, freckled face, with hair like burned straw.

The boy said, "Maw, can't I go out? Maw, can't a body go out and play?"

The woman ignored him; she was studying a book that was yellow with age. A girl stood looking over her shoulder at the book. The girl might have been a little older than the boy—or perhaps his twin; she was the same height.

The boy tried again, "Maw, lemme out."

A child of two years, toddling on the cabin floor, glanced at the boy with interest. Then he spoke his brother's name, "Josh."

A man lay on one of the beds that were built out from the cabin wall. He lay with a quilt drawn up to his chin, and in spite of the heat he seemed to be cold. Sometimes he moved a little, restlessly, but most of the time he lay still, only his eyes moving, watching the other people in the cabin.

Now he said, "Josh, you shut yore mouth! You leave your mom alone!"

The woman glanced up quickly from the book; her eyes met the man's, and she forced her face to smile. "Don't excite yourself," she said gently.

The man muttered something, lay back with his eyes closed. The boy crossed the cabin to the one window that had an open shutter. He stood there in a broad beam of sunlight.

"You get from there!" his mother said. She reached out a hand, but he dodged nimbly. He went over to the crib and began to play with the baby.

Drawing up her legs, the baby only whimpered louder. Sometimes she liked to play with the boy, but now her only desire was for her mother's milk. The boy snorted with disgust, and his eyes turned eagerly to the open window.

Beyond the window there showed a piece of cultivated ground, a cornfield and waves of ripe wheat, beyond that a stretch of forest. The boy could hear a brook gurgling, and he was thirsty. He thought of how it would be to roll all naked in the brook.

The woman sighed and closed the book. On its cover was printed: *Selde's Anatomy and Household Remedies: Boston, 1770.*

The girl, deprived of the book's fascination, wandered listlessly about the cabin.

When she stopped at the window, the mother snapped, "Get from that window!" But wearily, as if she had said it too many times.

The baby clamored for attention and milk.

"She makes me sick," Josh muttered.

The woman's eyes fixed on him, and he slipped into a corner, alongside the fireplace that dominated a whole wall of the cabin. He sulked there, reaching out curious fingers toward a large clean-bore musket that leaned against the stone.

The woman rose, went to the bed, and leaned over the man. He opened his eyes. She said, "I thought you were sleeping, Jemmy."

"No—I'm hot, hot like fire. You reckon I need stay covered?"

The boy and the girl were staring at him now, with some curiosity and a little fear. The woman rested her hand on the man's forehead.

"Fever, Sarah?"

"No fever." She smiled, then sat down on the bed beside him. But his eyes told her that he didn't believe, and she felt a strange, wilting fear. She glanced around the cabin.

Josh was fooling with the musket. She said, "Josh, you leave that musket alone! You'll be the death of me yet."

"Was there anything in the book to lead you on?" the man asked hesitantly. He twisted himself to face her, and then groaned with pain. He was a big, strong man, suffering doubly, the way a strong man does when strength suddenly leaves him. He had dark hair, but the same light blue eyes as the boy; his face was brown from the sun, but bloodless.

"There ain't a lot about gunshot wounds," the woman told him.

"It said nothing about the bullet being inside?"

She shook her head.

"My pa, he fought in the French war, in Canada. He said a man could take his death, leaving the lead inside of him."

"That ain't so!" she said.

At the word *death*, the girl began to cry.

The mother said, "You, Susie—stop that!"

"She ain't much," Josh remarked. "She's plenty scared, all right."

The baby was crying again. "I'll have to nurse her," Sarah muttered. "I'm straight nervous, but I'll have to nurse her."

The man whispered, "I don't want to be a load, Sarah, but I'm dreadful hot and thirsty. There's water?"

"Plenty of water." She went to the water jug, and his eyes followed her. She held a pewter cup to the opening, but the water stopped flowing before the cup was full.

The girl screamed, "Maw—Maw, gimme a drink of water!"

She had left the spigot open. A few drops trickled out, fell on the floor, and were absorbed immediately by the packed dirt.

The man had seen; holding himself up on one elbow, he stared at the water keg with wide blue eyes. Then he dropped back on the bed.

Her face impassive, the woman brought the cup of water over to him. He shook his head.

"Please," she begged, "drink it down, Jemmy. There's plenty more water. There's a pot of water I put away for boiling, and a pailful I was thinking to wash the children with."

She lied well; she lied the way only a woman can, when the lie will save, but he knew that she was lying.

Susie began, "Maw, please—" and then saw her mother's face and shrank back. The two-year-old balanced himself over the crib, and the baby stopped her whimpering for a moment to stare into her brother's eyes.

Then, for that moment, it was very still, the only sound being the gurgling of the brook just within the shade of the forest.

The mother's voice had dropped to a hoarse whisper. "For God's sake, Jemmy, drink this."

He didn't answer, only lay there with his eyes closed. The two-year-old had tired of watching the baby, and was now poking gingerly at her ribs. The baby began to scream.

"Leave her alone!"

Susie's eyes were on the cup of water. It was late in the afternoon now, and she had had nothing to drink since the morning. She was very, very thirsty. She took a step toward her mother. Josh had stood up and was staring at the window. Now the gurgling of the brook seemed louder than ever.

The mother bent over her husband and touched his face. It was very hot, and there were little beads of sweat all over it. It was a face that she knew and had known for twelve years, every line upon it, every hard fold of the skin. The cheeks were high and the jaw was large and gentle at the same time, a stubble of beard over it. Yet the face was different, and for a moment she imagined that he was dead.

"Jemmy, Jemmy," she pleaded.

Then he opened his eyes.

She held the water toward him, and even though he shook his head, she was relieved. With a few drops of the water she wet his face, and then she gave the rest to Susie.

At first, the girl stared at it and wouldn't drink; but the expression on her mother's face had changed. The woman was not beautiful, or even fair. Her face was too hard and too worn. But now the face was gentle with thankfulness.

The girl gulped down the water.

Josh said, "You let her drink—I don't get no water, but you let her drink."

"Yer a boy. I reckon you can stand a few hours without makin' a pig of yourself over water."

She went to the window, stood just to one side of it, and peered out. There was no living thing out there, nothing but the wheat and the corn and the green wall of forest. That was what made it so hard, not knowing. Yet she knew what might be out there, and of the cunning and the patience of what might be there.

The sun had dropped low, and now it was just over the forest's edge, throwing a shadow onto the wheat. A wind had come up with the evening, stirring the wheat. But no life. She knew the way a wind stirred the wheat.

She stood there for a while, glancing back into the cabin every now and then and wondering how it would be. Sooner or later it would come to a head. They would leave the cabin—or what waited out there in the forest would come and investigate the still cabin. The musket would be fired once, and then it would be over.

The water didn't make too much difference. It aggravated the situation, but in the end it would be the same.

Her husband said, "There wouldn't be no sign of them, Sarah."

"I know." She shrugged.

She went over to the bed, lifted the cover, and looked at his wound. She held herself so that the children wouldn't see.

Living this way, all in one room, it was a strange life. Not that she complained, thinking only that this was a way of transition, that someday this land would be like the land she had left behind in the East, on the other side of the mountains. Yet it was a strange life, all of them in one room, morning, noon, and night.

The wound was in his side, toward the front. He had not coughed any blood, so there was a good chance that his lungs were untouched. Yet the large, gaping hole was red and inflamed. She had treated it the only way she knew, stuffed it full of wet tobacco leaf.

He said, "I hardly felt it at first, like being hit in the side with a bit of rock."

Then, when he would have looked at it, she put back the dressing and covered him.

"It ain't no wound for a man to fret on," he said. "I'll be up outa bed maybe tomorrow, maybe come another sunset."

Then their eyes met. They trusted each other. She realized that trust was what had drawn them westward, where no sane persons would go.

He whispered, "Boone's stockade is west by north—sixty, seventy miles." Then he closed his eyes, and she sat by his bed, wondering. West by north—sixty or seventy miles.

Josh and his sister had crept to the open window; they stood there, peering out and trembling with excitement.

His mother's hand caught him over the ear.

"I don't see no Injuns, Maw."

"You stay from that window!"

She began to set out things for supper. Some salted meat —that would make them thirsty. There was corn on the cob, which she had boiled the day before. She wondered whether to give them the meat. If the cow were only in the house, they could have milk for a day at least. But the cow had wandered away.

She gave them the corn and held back the meat. Some of the corn she mashed up for her husband, but he was asleep when she went to him. She didn't want to wake him.

Josh complained about the food.

"Eat it," she said.

"Why can't we have meat, Maw?"

"Time the school was getting out here," she said. "It's a waste of a body's strength to live in a land without a school. You-all need a taste of a schoolmaster's rod."

The two-year-old ate with difficulty. He needed water, but he didn't complain. There was something solid about him, something that reminded her of his father. He had his father's name. Josh's mouth was swollen and dry.

She nursed the baby. She sat in the corner, just within the bulge of the fireplace. There was a sort of peace now, Josh and his sister sitting at the table, talking in low tones.

The baby gave up the breast and began to whimper again. Sarah realized that she was dry, all dry, inside and outside. Her mouth was like bad-tasting leather. If it was that way with her, how was it with the children? Before morning came, Jemmy would die. More than anything else, he had to have water.

She put the child back in his crib. Then she went to the window and stared out at the forest. All in the shade now; the sun was setting. A wide band of shadow bordered the forest.

She took down a wooden water pail, stared at it a moment, and set it on the table. She could go herself—Josh was looking at her. If I don't come back . . . she thought.

She said to Josh, "If I sent you down to the brook for water, you'd come right back?"

He nodded eagerly.

"You know how with Pa? Pa was shot. They're out there, waitin'. You know that?"

He nodded again.

She couldn't say any more. Her throat was tight inside and her heart was a heavy lump in her breast. She gave Josh the pail, all the while wondering what impelled her to do it. And then, at the last moment, she would have kept him back. "Walk," she said. "Don't run—walk."

He nodded soberly. She opened the door, reached to touch him, and then held herself back. Now it seemed to her that this was the culmination of her life, and that more than this she could not be called upon to do.

A waving track in the corn marked his path. In the wheat, he showed again, head and shoulders, and then he was lost in the shadow of the forest.

Sarah felt the girl, close to her, ordered her back into the house. Then it seemed to her that she had been standing there for hours, in the doorway—waiting.

There were sounds from the forest now, where there had been no sound before. Or else it was her mind, making sounds for her to be afraid of.

The baby was whimpering again. Her feet were like lead when she went inside, soothed her. If Jemmy woke up and saw that Josh had gone—Josh was his first man-child, a thing to be proud of and called after Jemmy's own father.

She went back to the door. The shadow of the forest had crept out further; it was twilight now.

She saw him in the wheat, head and shoulders. Then she wanted to run forward and meet him; and somehow she held back. When he came out of the corn, he wasn't running—walking as she had said and bearing the pail of water carefully.

The shot from the forest was like the snapping of a dry piece of wood, not terribly loud, but ringing afterward, as if someone had fired again and again. The pail of water in the boy's hand shattered to pieces, splashing him. He ran forward to the house, and she bolted the door behind him. Then she was down on her knees, feeling all over him with her rough hand, which she tried so desperately to make gentle.

He was crying a little. There was a splinter in his arm, and he winced when she drew it out. His arm was bruised, but otherwise he wasn't hurt.

Jemmy was awake, staring at them. She couldn't be sure, because now the cabin was almost dark, but she imagined that there was no reason in his eyes.

Josh said, "I didn't drink, I swear, Maw—I didn't drink at the crick."

"I know, I know, child."

"You want me to go back, Maw?"

"No—no." She was thinking of what Jemmy would say, knowing that she had sent Josh down there alone.

She went to the single window that was open, closed it, and bolted the shutter. Then she scraped flint and steel until a candle was lit. The baby was sleeping, and she was thankful for that. It was a wonder that she could sleep through it. The two-year-old sat on the floor, playing with a piece of wood. Susie was close to Josh, hardly knowing whether to cry or not.

Jemmy was awake. She saw his eyes as soon as she lit the candle, and she saw that he didn't know. Staring straight at her, he didn't see her. He was repeating what he had told her that morning, when he had come back to the cabin, all wet with blood and barely able to walk, "I was breaking open the land down the crick bottom. I didn't hear a sound, only the first thing I knew there's a pain in my side, like someone threw a rock at me. Funny about not hearing a shot, just a pain in my side, and then the red devil running at me. I split him with the ax, but there's more. Reckon you kin count on there being plenty more of them holed up here. I got a mortal hurt, Sarah."

The boy and the girl were listening, their eyes wide with horror. Susie crept up to Josh, and he put his arm around her. She was crying a little, and Josh said, "That ain't no way to carry on."

"Come to bed," Sarah told them, just as if she had heard nothing, and when Jemmy moaned again and again, she made out that it was nothing for the children to be worried over.

The two-year-old slept thankfully and quietly, but it hurt

Sarah to see how swollen his mouth was, eyes bloodshot.
Josh and his sister slept together in the same bed. There, in
the shadow, they became disembodied whispers. Sarah
hoped they would sleep soon.

"It's a long way north and west," Jemmy mumbled.
"Boone's a fine man and easy to take in strangers. But long
walking—for sixty miles. The canebrake ain't easy in summer heat."

Sarah took up the candle and walked around the cabin,
from window to window, making sure that the shutters on
each were bolted. At the fireplace, she stopped, poking at
the ashes. She had heard of a cabin on the River Licking,
where they had dropped down the chimney to invade the
place. It might be wise for her to start a fire, only in this
heat it would make a furnace of the cabin. They wouldn't
sleep with a fire in the cabin.

She took the candle in her hand and stood by Jemmy's
bed. He had thrown off his covers, and when she drew them
back he opened his eyes and looked straight at her without
seeing her. She wiped the beads of sweat from his face.

"The road to the West is a way of darkness," he whispered. "God help me for going where no man stepped before."

"Sleep, Jemmy," she begged him.

He grasped for her hand. "There's no way out of this.
I'm awful hot!" He had hesitated, closed his eyes for a
while. She still stood by the bed.

"Where's Josh?" he asked her.

"Sleeping."

"I had a dream that he went. I heard a shot fired. Let
me up!" He struggled erect, clawed his way from the bed,
and sprawled on the floor. She had a time getting him back

into the bed. His body had relaxed, and he was whimpering like a child.

After that, she sat by the table for a long time, just sat and stared straight in front of her.

She was very, very tired, and she was priming herself for an effort that would keep her awake through the night. Somehow, she had to manage to remain awake.

When she went to Jemmy's bed again, he was sleeping. She took the candle and looked at the children. Josh was sprawled the way a child sleeps in hot weather, arms and legs flung out, his face buried in the pillow. She bent over Josh, made as if to touch him, and then drew back her hand. Susie lay on her back, her soft hair like silver over her face. Sarah put the hair away, strand by strand.

Back at the table, she might have dozed for a moment or an hour. She didn't know as she started awake in the dark. The candle had burned out, and something was scratching at the door.

At first, the darkness frightened and stifled her. She had a sensation of being alone in a world of mystery, in a black world that stretched north and south and east and west for more miles than a man could count. Then, in that moment— fearfully—she lived over the great distance they had come from the East, the mountain passes, the gorges, the mysterious forest that stretched on and on, the sense of going into the wild, where man's law and man's mercy stopped.

She had somehow stumbled across the room and found the musket. She stood in the corner, holding it before her, feeling for the trigger. She felt that when she pulled the trigger, the crash of the gun would mark the end of all that had been for them. That way she waited, her eyes fixed on the place where the door was.

The scratching continued, and once she imagined that she heard steps outside. And then she felt that someone out there was listening.

It required all her courage to clink the gun metal against the stone of the fireplace. That was what they were listening for, and she'd let them hear it. Then she raised the lock of the gun. In the night, the noise was magnified—unmistakably the sound of a musket being cocked.

And after that, for a long time, silence.

She was wet all over; drops of water running down her face splashed onto her hands. When she put the musket away, it was with a distinct effort that she unclasped her hands from the moist stock and barrel.

At the table, she found a candle, flint and steel, and tried to make a light. Her hands trembled, and again and again she dropped the flint or the steel. Finally, she had the tinder glowing, and the candlewick flickered into life. The light was a benediction and a caress.

The baby was crying. Sarah took her up in her arms, soothed her, and began to nurse. A wind had raised itself outside, and the sound of it reminded Sarah of a lullaby her own mother had sung. That was in another world. Perhaps this child would go on that way, westward, as she had gone.

She nursed until the girl slept, and then she sat there with the child in her arms. Jemmy awakened; she didn't notice at first, until she saw him sitting up in bed, looking at her.

He said, "Sarah, it's morning?"

"Soon, Jemmy."

"Why don't you get some sleep?"

"I slept a spell before. I'm all right, Jemmy." She knew that he wanted her to come to him and she put the child back in her crib. Next to Jemmy, she passed her hand over his face; it was cooler now.

"I woke up before," he whispered. "It was dark. I thought—"

"No, the candle went out, Jemmy."

"I been thinkin'," he said.

"Rest, Jemmy."

He said, "I been thinkin' for you to slip out—find Boone. They won't leave the cabin, an' tomorrow they'll close in. Take the kids."

"Leave you here?"

"I'm a man shot through; I ain't no good. You're a strong woman an' you need a strong man. Find Boone, an' find a man to marry an' fetch you food—"

"You'll be better, Jemmy."

He turned over with his face to the wall. She felt under the blanket, found his hand, and held it. He had large hands, hard and broken with callus. She tried to understand how the hand could be shorn of strength; everything had come with his hands, even the house they lived in.

She left the bed, sat down at the table again, staring at the candle and wondering idly whether it would burn till morning. She watched it until it had flickered out. Through the crevices in the windows, a gray harbinger of dawn filtered in.

She was filled with an almost childish amazement at the fact that another day had come. It was not yet light enough in the cabin to see anything else than vague shapes.

From bed to bed she looked at each of her children. She bent low over Jemmy, the two-year-old, saw that there was a sort of smile on his face. She kissed him and said to herself, "He'll have schoolin' anyhow. Seems there's bound to

be a day when the school'll come away out here. I'd like
a school and a church and a preacher. It don't seem right
a boy should grow to man's age without listening to a
preacher."

Then she sat herself in a chair and prayed, silently. Even
with the others sleeping, her reserve was too much for her
to pray aloud.

After that, when the noise came at the door again, she
didn't care so much, nor was she frightened, the way she
had been before. With the dawn, a strange peace had come
over her.

She took up the baby in her arms and stood waiting.
Someone was pounding at the door.

A white man's voice cried, "Halloo in there!"

She was sobbing, not tears but a heaving inside of her
that she felt would rack her apart. She had only enough
strength to unbolt the door, and then she dropped into a
chair and watched them flood into the room with the gray
light of dawn—many tall men in long homespun shirts,
carrying rifles.

They filled the cabin, full and overflowing. They were
big men and the cabin was small. They spoke in full,
throaty voices, grinned at her, and petted the baby.

Josh and Susie woke, frightened at first, but in a little
while Josh was telling them how the water bucket had been
shot out of his hand.

The man they called Dan'l spoke to her, a stocky man
who was not very tall, yet gave an impression of great size
and easy strength. He said, "My name's Boone, ma'am—
I'm mighty proud to meet you." He took up the baby, fon-
dled it with hands that were wonderfully gentle. "It's a fine
girl," he said.

She was holding Susie, touching her hair and explaining, "My man was shot—down in the creek bottom, an Indian. There's a doctor with you?"

"I have a way in healing—a small way."

Jemmy was awake, staring at them. Sarah was thinking, He's like them, tall and strong. He will be.

They gave her water, while Boone bent over Jemmy. She let the children drink first, slapped Josh for gulping. The taste of water on her own lips was like a dream.

Then she went to Boone, stood by his side while he dressed her husband's wound. "He's hurt bad?" she whispered.

Boone held the bullet between his fingers. "He'll mend soon enough. He'll be a strong man, walking and providing."

She dropped down on the bed, put her face in her hands. Jemmy's hand went out, found her arm and caressed it, the callus rough on her skin.

Boone said, "We'll bide here for a spell, until he's up and around. It's a hard task for a woman, minding a family and a sick man. Some of us will bide with you for a spell."

She looked at him, wide eyes in a hard face, but eyes that were soft with knowing. "Not too hard—" she said. "Forgive me, I'll sleep a little. I'm fair tired now." Then she lay down by her husband and closed her eyes.

MOUNTAIN MEDICINE

A. B. GUTHRIE, JR.

The mist along the creek shone in the morning sun, which was coming up lazy and halfhearted, as if of a mind to turn back and let the spring season wait. The cottonwoods and quaking aspens were still bare and the needles of the pines old and dark with winter, but beaver were prime and beaver were plenty. John Clell made a lift and took the drowned animal quietly from the trap and stretched it in the dugout with three others.

Bill Potter said, "If 'tweren't for the Injuns! Or if 'tweren't for you and your notions!" For all his bluster, he still spoke soft, as if on the chance that there were other ears to hear.

Clell didn't answer. He reset the trap and pulled from the mud the twig that slanted over it. Then he unstoppered his goat-horn medicine bottle, dipped the twig in it, and poked it back into the mud.

"Sometimes I think you're scary," Potter went on, studying Clell out of eyes that were small and set close. "What kind of medicine is it makes you smell Injuns with nary one about?"

"Time you see as many of them as I have, you'll be scary too," Clell answered, slipping his paddle into the stream. He had a notion to get this greenhorn told off, but he let it slide. What was the use? You couldn't put into a greenhorn's head what it was you felt. You couldn't give him the feel of distances and sky-high mountains and lonely winds and ideas spoken out of nowhere, ideas spoken into the head by medicines a man couldn't put a name to. Like now. Like here. Like this idea that there was brown skin about, and Blackfoot skin at that.

"I seen Blackfeet enough for both of us," he added. His mind ran back to Lewis and Clark and a time that seemed long ago because so much had come between; to days and nights and seasons of watching out, with just himself and the long silence for company; to last year and a hole that lay across the mountains to the south, where the Blackfeet and the Crows had fought, and he had sided with the

Crows and got a wound in the leg that hurt sometimes yet. He could still see some of the Blackfeet faces. He would know them, and they would know him, being long-remembering.

He knew Blackfeet all right, but he couldn't tell Bill Potter why he thought some of them were close by. There wasn't any sign he could point to; the creek sang along and the breeze played in the trees, and overhead a big eagle was gliding low, and nowhere was there a footprint or movement or a whiff of smoke. It was just a feeling he had, and Potter wouldn't understand it, but would only look at him and maybe smile with one side of his mouth.

"Ain't anybody I knows of carries a two-shoot gun but you," Potter said, still talking as if Clell was scared over nothing.

Clell looked down at it, where he had it angled to his hand. It had two barrels, fixed on a swivel. When the top one was fired, you slipped a catch and turned the other up. One barrel was rifled, the other bigger and smooth-bored, and sometimes he loaded the big one with shot, for birds, and sometimes with a heavy ball, for bear or buffalo, or maybe with ball and buck both. There was shot in it this morning, for he had thought maybe to take ducks or geese, and so refresh his taste for buffalo meat. The rifle shone in the morning sun. It was a nice piece, with a patch box a man wouldn't know to open until someone showed him the place to press his thumb. For no reason at all, Clell called his rifle Mule Ear.

He said, "You're a fool, Potter, more ways than one. Injuns'll raise your hair for sure, if it don't so happen I do it myself. As for this here two-shooter, I like it, and that's that."

Bill Potter always took low when a man dared him like that. Now all he said was "It's too heavy."

Slipping along the stream, with the banks rising steep on both sides, Clell thought about beaver and Indians and all the country he had seen—high country, pretty as paint, wild as any animal and lonesome as time, and rivers unseen but by him, and holes and creeks without a name, and one place where water spouted hot and steaming and sometimes stinking from the earth, and another where a big spring flowed with pure tar; and no one believed him when he told of them, but called him the biggest liar yet. It was all right, though. He knew what he knew, and kept it to himself now, being tired of queer looks and smiles and words that made out he was half-crazy.

Sometimes, remembering things, he didn't see what people did or hear what they said or think to speak when spoken to. It was all right. It didn't matter what was said about his sayings or his doings or his ways of thinking. A man long alone where no other white foot ever stepped got different. He came to know what the Indians meant by medicine. He got to feeling like one with the mountains and the great sky and the lonesome winds and the animals and Indians, too, and it was a little as if he knew what they knew, a little as if there couldn't be a secret but was whispered to him, like the secret he kept hearing now.

"Let's cache," he said to Potter. The mist was gone from the river and the sun well up and decided on its course. It was time, and past time, to slide back to their hidden camp.

"Just got one more trap to lift," Potter argued.

"All right, then."

Overhead the eagle still soared close. Clell heard its long, high cry. He heard something else, too, a muffled pounding

of feet on the banks above. "Injuns!" he said, and bent the
canoe into the cover of an overhanging bush. "I told you."

Potter listened. "Buffalo is all. Buffalo trampin' around."

Clell couldn't be sure, except for the feeling in him.
Down in this little canyon a man couldn't see to the banks
above. It could be buffalo, all right, but something kept
warning, "Injuns! Injuns!"

Potter said, "Let's git on. Can't be cachin' from every
little noise. Even sparrers make noise."

"Wait a spell."

"Scary." Potter said just the one word, and he said it under
his breath, but it was enough. Clell dipped his paddle. One
day he would whip Potter, but right now he reckoned he
had to go on.

It wasn't fear that came on him a shake later, but just
the quick knowing he had been right all along, just the
holding still, the waiting, the watching what to do, for the
banks had broken out with Indians—Indians with feathers
in their hair, and bows and war clubs and spears in their
hands; Indians yelling and motioning and scrambling down
to the shores on both sides and fitting arrows to their bowstrings.

Potter's face had gone white and tight like rawhide drying. He grabbed at his rifle.

Clell said, "Steady!" and got the pipe that hung from
around his neck and held it up, meaning he meant peace.

These were the Blackfeet sure enough. These were the
meanest Indians living. He would know them from the Rees
and Crows and Pierced Noses and any other. He would
know them by their round heads and bent noses and their
red-and-green leather shields and the moccasins mis-

matched in color, and their bows and robes not fancy, and no man naked in the bunch.

The Indians waved them in. Clell let go his pipe and stroked with his paddle. Potter's voice was shrill. "You fool! You gonna let 'em torment us to death?"

That was the way with a mouthy greenhorn—full of himself at first, and then wild and shaken. "Steady!" Clell said again. "I aim to pull to shore. Don't point that there rifle 'less you want a skinful of arrows."

There wasn't a gun among the Indians, not a decent gun, but only a few rusty trade muskets. They had battle-axes, and bows taken from their cases, ready for business, and some had spears, and all looked itching for a white man's hair. They waited, their eyes bright as buttons, their faces and bare forearms and right shoulders shining brown in the sun. Only men were at the shore line, but Clell could see the faces of squaws and young ones looking down from the bank above.

An Indian splashed out and got hold of the prow of the canoe and pulled it in. Clell stepped ashore, holding up his pipe. He had to watch Potter. Potter stumbled out, his little eyes wide and his face white, and fear showing even for an Indian to see. When he stepped onto the bank, one of the Indians grabbed his rifle and wrenched it from him, and Potter just stood like a scared rabbit, looking as if he might jump back in the dugout any minute.

Clell reached out and took a quick hold on the rifle and jerked it away and handed it back to Potter. There was a way to treat Indians. Act like a squaw and they treated you bad; act like a brave man and you might have a chance.

Potter snatched the gun and spun around and leaped.

The force of the jump carried the canoe out. He made a splash with the paddle. An arrow whispered in the air and made a little thump when it hit. Clell saw the end of it, shaking from high in Potter's back.

Potter cried out, "I'm hit! I'm hit, Clell!"

"Come back! Easy! Can't get away!"

Instead Potter swung around with the rifle. There were two sounds, the crack of the powder and the gunshot plunk of a ball. Clell caught a glimpse of an Indian going down, and then the air was full of the twang of bowstrings and the whispered flight of arrows, and Potter slumped slowly back in the canoe, his body stuck like a pincushion. An Indian splashed out to take the scalp. Two others carried the shot warrior up the bank. Already a squaw was beginning to keen.

Clell stood quiet as a stump, letting only his eyes move. It was so close now that his life was as good as gone. He could see it in the eyes around him, in the hungry faces, in the hands moving and the spears and the bows being raised. He stood straight, looking their eyes down, thinking the first arrow would come any time now, and from any place, and then he heard the eagle scream. Its shadow lazed along the ground. His thumb slipped the barrel catch, his wrist twisted under side up. He shot without knowing he aimed. Two feathers puffed out of the bird. It went into a steep climb and faltered and turned head down and spun to the ground, making a thump when it hit.

The Indians' eyes switched back to him. Their mouths fell open, and slowly their hands came over the mouth holes in the sign of surprise. It was as he figured in that flash between life and death. They thought all guns fired a single ball. They thought he was big medicine as a marksman. One of them stepped out and laid his hand on Mule Ear, as if to draw some of its greatness into himself. A murmur started up, growing into an argument. They ordered Clell up the bank. When he got there, he saw one Indian high-tailing it for the eagle, and others following, so's to have plumes for their war bonnets, maybe, or to eat the raw flesh for the medicine it would give them.

There was a passel of Indians on the bank, three or four hundred, and more coming across from the other side. The man Clell took for the chief had mixed red earth with spit and dabbed it on his face. He carried a bird-wing fan in one hand and wore a half-sleeved hunting shirt made of bighorn skin and decorated with colored porcupine quills. His hair was a wild bush over his eyes and ears. At the back of it he had a tuft of owl feathers hanging. He yelled something and motioned with his hands, and the others began drifting back from the bank, except for a couple of dozen that Clell figured were headmen. Mostly, they wore leggings and moccasins, and leather shirts or robes slung over the left shoulder. A few had scarlet trade blankets, which had come from who knew where. One didn't wear anything under his robe.

The squaws and the little squaws in their leather sacks of dresses, the naked boys with their potbellies and swollen navels, and the untried and middling warriors were all back now. The chief and the rest squatted down in a half circle, with Clell standing in front of them. They passed a pipe around. After a while they began to talk. He had some of the hang of Blackfoot, and he knew, even without their words, they were arguing what to do with him. One of them got up and came over and brought his face close to Clell's. His eyes picked at Clell's head and eyes and nose and mouth. Clell could smell grease on him and wood smoke and old sweat, but what came to his mind above all was that here was a man he had fought last season while siding with the Crows. He looked steadily into the black eyes and saw the knowing come into them, too, and watched the man turn back and take his place in the half circle and heard him telling what he knew.

They grunted like hogs, the Blackfeet did, like hogs about to be fed, while the one talked and pointed, arguing that here was a friend of their old enemies, the Crows. The man rubbed one palm over the other, saying in sign that Clell had to be rubbed out. Let them stand up and use him for a target, the man said. The others said yes to that, not nodding their heads as white men would, but bowing forward and back from the waist.

Clell had just one trick left. He stepped over and showed his gun and pointed to the patch box and, waving one hand to catch their eyes, he sprang the cover with the other thumb. He closed the cover and handed the gun to the chief.

The chief's hands were red with the paint he had smeared on his face. Clell watched the long thumbnail, hooked like a bird claw, digging at the cover, watched the red fingers feeling for the latch or spring. While the others stretched their necks to see, the chief turned Mule Ear over, prying at it with his eyes. It wasn't any use. Unless he knew the hidden spot to press, he couldn't spring the lid. Clell took the piece back, opened the patch box again, closed it, and sat down.

He couldn't make more medicine. He didn't have a glass to bring the sun down, and so to light a pipe, or even a trader's paper-backed mirror for the chief to see how pretty he was. All he had was the shot at the eagle and the patch box on Mule Ear, and he had used them both and had to take what came.

Maybe it was the eagle that did it, or the hidden cover, or maybe it was just the crazy way of Indians. The chief got up, and with his hands and with his tongue asked if the white hunter was a good runner.

Clell took his time answering, as a man did when making high palaver. He lighted his pipe. He said, "The white hunter is a bad runner. The other Long Knives think he runs fast. Their legs are round from sitting on a horse. They cannot run."

The chief grunted, letting the sign talk and the slow words sink into him. "The Long Knife will run." He pointed to the south, away from the creek. "He will run for the trading house that the whiteface keeps among the Crows. He will go as far as three arrows will shoot, and then he will run. My brothers will run. If my brothers run faster—" The chief brought his hand to his scalp lock.

The other Indians had gathered around, even the squaws and the young ones. They were grunting with excitement. The chief took Mule Ear. Other hands stripped off Clell's hunting shirt, the red-checked woolen shirt underneath, his leggings, his moccasins, his smallclothes, until he stood white and naked in the sun, and the squaws and young ones came up close to see what white flesh looked like. The squaws made little noises in their throats. They poked at his bare hide. One of them grabbed the red-checked shirt from the hands of a man and ran off with it. The chief made the sign for "Go!"

Clell walked straight, quartering into the sun. He walked slow and solemn, like going to church. If he hurried, they would start the chase right off. If he lazed along, making out he didn't care, they might give him more of a start.

He was two hundred yards away when the first whoop sounded, the first single whoop, and then all the voices yelling and making one great whoop. From the corner of his eyes he saw their legs driving, saw the uncovered brown skins, the feathered hair, the bows and spears, and then he was running himself, seeing ahead of him the far tumble and roll of high plains and hills, with buffalo dotting the distances and a herd of prairie goats sliding like summer mist, and everywhere, so that not always could his feet miss them, the angry knobs of cactus. South and east, many a long camp away where the Big Horn joined the Yellowstone, lay Lisa's Fort, the trading house among the Crows.

He ran so as to save himself from running, striding long and loose through the new-sprouting buffalo grass, around the cactus, around pieces of sandstone where snakes were likely to lie. He made himself breathe easy, breathe deep, breathe full in his belly. Far off in his feelings he felt the cactus sting him and the spines pull off to sting again. The sun looked him in the face. It lay long and warm on the world. At the sky line the heat sent up a little shimmer. There wasn't a noise anywhere except the thump of his feet and his heart working in his chest and his breath sucking in and out and, behind him, a cry now and then from the Indians, seeming not closer or farther away than at first. He couldn't slow himself with a look. He began to sweat.

A man could run a mile, or two or three, and then his breath wheezed in him. It grew into a hard snore in the throat. The air came in, weak and dry, and burned his pipes and went out in one spent rush while his lungs sucked for more. He felt as if he had been running on forever. He felt strange and out of the world, a man running in a dream, except that the ache in his throat was real and the fire of cactus in his feet. The earth spread away forever, and he was lost in it and friendless, and not a proper part of it any more; and it served him right. When a man didn't pay any mind to his medicine, but went ahead regardless, as he had done, his medicine played out on him.

Clell looked back. He had gained—fifty yards, seventy-five, half a musket shot; he had gained on all the Indians except one, and that one ran as swift and high-headed as a prairie goat. He was close and coming closer.

Clell had a quick notion to stop and fight. He had an idea he might dodge the spear the Indian carried and come to grips with him. But the rest would be on him before he finished. It took time to kill a man just with the hands alone. Now was the time for the running he had saved himself for. There was strength in his legs yet. He made them reach out, farther, faster, faster, farther. The pound of them came to be a sick jolting inside his skull. His whole chest fought for air through the hot, closed tunnel of his throat. His legs weren't a part of him; they were something to think about, but not to feel, something to watch and to wonder at. He saw them come out and go under him and come out again. He saw them weakening, the knees bending in a little as the weight came on them. He felt wetness on his face, and reached up and found his nose was streaming blood.

He looked over his shoulder again. The main body of Indians had fallen farther back, but the prairie goat had gained. Through a fog he saw the man's face, the chin set high and hard, the black eyes gleaming. He heard the moccasins slapping in the grass.

Of a sudden, Clell made up his mind. Keep on running and he'd get a spear in the back. Let it come from the front. Let it come through the chest. Let him face up to death like a natural man. His feet jolted him to a halt. He swung around and threw up his hands as if to stop a brute.

The Indian wasn't ready for that. He tried to pull up quick. He made to lift his spear. And then he stumbled and fell ahead. The spear handle broke as the point dug into the ground. Clell grabbed at the shaft, wrenched the point from the earth, and drove it through the man. The Indian bucked to his hands and knees and strained and sank back. It was as easy as that.

Bending over him, Clell let his chest drink, let his numb legs rest, until he heard the yells of the Indians and, looking up, saw them strung in a long file, with the closest of them so close he could see the set of their faces. He turned and ran again, hearing a sudden, louder howling as the Indians came on the dead one, and then the howling dying again to single cries as they picked up the chase. They were too many for him, and too close. He didn't have a chance. He couldn't fort up and try to stand them off, not with his hands bare. There wasn't any place to hide. He should have listened to his medicine when it was talking to him back there on the creek.

Down the slope ahead of him a river ran—the Jefferson Fork of the Missouri, he thought, while he made his legs drive him through a screen of brush. A beaver swam in the river, its moving head making a quiet V in the still water above a dam. As he pounded closer, its flat tail slapped the water like a pistol shot, the point of the V sank from sight, and the ripples spread out and lost themselves. He could still see the beaver, though, swimming under water, its legs moving and the black tail plain, like something to follow. It was a big beaver, and it was making for a beaver lodge at Clell's right.

Clell dived, came up gasping from the chill of mountain water, and started stroking for the other shore. Beaver lodge! Beaver lodge! It was as if something spoke to him, as if someone nudged him, as if the black tail pulled him around. It was a fool thing, swimming under water and feeling for the tunnel that led up into the lodge. A fool thing. A man got so winded and weak that he didn't know medicine from craziness. A fool thing. A man couldn't force his shoulders through a beaver hole. The point of his shoulder pushed into mud. A snag ripped his side. He clawed ahead, his lungs bursting. And then his head was out of water, in the dark, and his lungs pumped air.

He heard movement in the lodge and a soft churring, but his eyes couldn't see anything. He pulled himself up, still hearing the churring, expecting the quick slice of teeth in his flesh. There was a scramble. Something slid along his leg and made a splash in the water of the tunnel, and slid again and made another splash.

His hands felt sticks and smooth, dry mud and the softness of shed hair. He sat up. The roof of the lodge just cleared his head if he sat slouched. It was a big lodge, farther across than the span of his arms. And it was as dark, almost, as the inside of a plugged barrel. His hand crossing before his eyes was just a shapeless movement.

He sat still and listened. The voices of the Indians sounded far off. He heard their feet in the stream, heard the moccasins walking softly around the lodge, heard the crunch of dried grass under their steps. It was like something dreamed, this hiding and being able to listen and to move. It was like being a breath of air, and no one able to put a hand on it.

After a while the footsteps trailed off and the voices faded. Now Clell's eyes were used to blackness, the lodge was a dark dapple. From the shades he would know when it was day, but that was all. He felt for the cactus spines in his feet. He had been cold and wet at first, but the wetness dried and the lodge warmed a little to his body. Shivering, he lay down, feeling the dried mud under his skin, and the soft fur. When he closed his eyes he could see the sweep of distances and the high climb of mountains, and himself all alone in all the world, and, closer up, he could see the beaver swimming under water and its flat tail beckoning. He could hear voices, the silent voices speaking to a lonesome man out of nowhere and out of everywhere, and the beaver speaking, too, the smack of its tail speaking.

He woke up later, quick with alarm, digging at his dream and the noise that had got mixed with it. It was night outside. Not even the dark dapple showed inside the lodge, but only such a blackness as made a man feel himself to make sure he was real. Then he heard a snuffling of the air, and the sound of little waves lapping in the tunnel, and he knew that a beaver had nosed up and smelled him and drawn back into the water.

When he figured it was day, he sat up slowly, easing his muscles into action. He knew, without seeing, that his feet were puffed with the poison of the cactus. He crawled to the tunnel and filled his lungs and squirmed into it. He came up easy, just letting his eyes and nose rise above the water. The sun had cleared the eastern sky line. Not a breath of air stirred; the earth lay still, flowing into spring. He could see where the Indians had flattened the grass and trampled an edging of rushes, but there were no Indians about, not on one side or the other, not from shore line to sky line. He struck out for the far shore.

Seven days later a hunter at Fort Lisa spotted a figure far off. He watched it for a long spell, until a mist came over his eyes, and then he called to the men inside the stockade. A half dozen came through the big gate, their rifles in the crooks of their arms, and stood outside and studied the figure, too.

"Man, all right. Somep'n ails him. Look how he goes."

"Injun, I say. A Crow, maybe, with a Blackfoot arrer in him."

"Git the glass."

One of them went inside and came back and put the glass to his eye. "Naked as a jay bird."

"Injun, ain't it?"

"Got a crop of whiskers. Never seen an Injun with whiskers yet."

"Skin's black."

"Ain't a Injun, though."

They waited.

"It ain't! Yes, I do believe it's John Clell! It's John Clell or I'm a Blackfoot!"

They brought him in and put his great, raw swellings of feet in hot water and gave him brandy and doled out roast liver, and bit by bit, that day and the next, he told them what had happened.

They knew why he wouldn't eat prairie turnips afterward, seeing as he lived on raw ones all that time, but what they didn't understand, because he didn't try to tell them, was why he never would hunt beaver again.

JACOB AND THE INDIANS

STEPHEN VINCENT BENÉT

It goes back to the early days—may God profit all who lived then—and the ancestors.

Well, America, you understand, in those days was different. It was a nice place, but you wouldn't believe it if you saw it today. Without buses, without trains, without States, without Presidents, nothing!

With nothing but colonies and Indians and wild woods all over the country and wild animals to live in the wild

woods. Imagine such a place! In these days, you children
don't even think about it; you read about it in the school-
books, but what is that? And I put in a call to my daughter,
in California, and in three minutes I am saying, "Hello,
Rosie," and there it is Rosie and she is telling me about the
weather, as if I wanted to know! But things were not always that way. I remember my own days, and they were
different. And in the times of my grandfather's grandfather,
they were different still. Listen to the story.

My grandfather's grandfather was Jacob Stein, and he
came from Rettelsheim, in Germany. To Philadelphia he
came, an orphan in a sailing ship, but not a common man.
He had learning—he had been to the *chedar*—he could
have been a scholar among the scholars. Well, that is the
way things happen in this bad world. There was a plague
and a new grand duke—things are always so. He would
say little of it afterward—they had left his teeth in his
mouth, but he would say little of it. He did not have to say
—we are children of the Dispersion, we know a black day
when it comes.

Yet, imagine—a young man with fine dreams and learning, a scholar with a pale face and narrow shoulders, set
down in those early days in such a new country. Well, he
must work, and he did. It was very fine, his learning, but
it did not fill his mouth. He must carry a pack on his back
and go from door to door with it. That was no disgrace; it
was so that many began. But it was not expounding the
law, and at first he was very homesick. He would sit in his
room at night, with the one candle, and read the preacher
Koheleth, till the bitterness of the preacher rose in his
mouth. Myself, I am sure that Koheleth was a great
preacher, but if he had had a good wife he would have

been a more cheerful man. They had too many wives in those old days—it confused them. But Jacob was young.

As for the new country where he had come, it was to him a place of exile, large and frightening. He was glad to be out of the ship, but, at first, that was all. And when he saw his first real Indian in the street—well, that was a day! But the Indian, a tame one, bought a ribbon from him by signs, and after that he felt better. Nevertheless, it seemed to him at times that the straps of the pack cut into his very soul, and he longed for the smell of the *chedar* and the quiet streets of Rettelsheim and the good smoked goose breast pious housewives kept for the scholar. But there is no going back—there is never any going back.

All the same, he was a polite young man and a hard worker. And soon he had a stroke of luck—or at first it seemed so. It was from Simon Ettelsohn that he got the trinkets for his pack, and one day he found Simon Ettelsohn arguing a point of the law with a friend, for Simon was a pious man and well-thought-of in the Congregation Mikveh Israel. Our grandfather's grandfather stood by very modestly at first—he had come to replenish his pack and Simon was his employer. But finally his heart moved within him, for both men were wrong, and he spoke and told them where they erred. For half an hour he spoke, with his pack still upon his shoulders, and never has a text been expounded with more complexity, not even by the great Reb Samuel. Till, in the end, Simon Ettelsohn threw up his hands and called him a young David and a candle of learning. Also, he allowed him a more profitable route of trade. But, best of all, he invited young Jacob to his house, and there Jacob ate well for the first time since he had come to Philadelphia. Also he laid eyes upon Miriam Ettelsohn for

JACOB AND THE INDIANS

the first time. She was Simon's youngest daughter and a rose of Zion.

After that, things went better for Jacob, for the protection of the strong is like a rock and a well. But yet things did not go altogether as he wished. For, at first, Simon Ettelsohn made much of him, and there was stuffed fish and raisin wine for the young scholar, though he was a peddler. But there is a look in a man's eyes that says, "H'm? Son-in-law?" and that look Jacob did not see. He was modest—he did not expect to win the maiden overnight, though he longed for her. But gradually it was borne in upon him what he was in the Ettelsohn house—a young scholar to be shown before Simon's friends, but a scholar whose learning did not fill his mouth. He did not blame Simon for it, but it was not what he had intended. He began to wonder if he would ever get on in the world at all, and that is not good for any man.

Nevertheless, he could have borne it, and the aches and pains of his love, had it not been for Meyer Kappelhuist. Now, there was a pushing man! I speak no ill of anyone, not even of your Aunt Cora, and she can keep the De Groot silver if she finds it in her heart to do so; who lies down in the straw with a dog, gets up with fleas. But this Meyer Kappelhuist! A big, red-faced fellow from Holland with shoulders the size of a barn door and red hair on the back of his hands. A big mouth for eating and drinking and telling *schnorrer* stories—and he talked about the Kappelhuists, in Holland, till you'd think they were made of gold. The crane says, "I am really a peacock—at least on my mother's side." And yet, a thriving man—that could not be denied. He had started with a pack, like our grandfather's grandfather, and now he was trading with the Indians and making money hand over fist. It seemed to Jacob that he could never go to the Ettelsohn house without meeting Meyer and hearing about those Indians. And it dried the words in Jacob's mouth and made his heart burn.

For no sooner would our grandfather begin to expound a text or a proverb than he would see Meyer Kappelhuist looking at the maiden. And when Jacob had finished his expounding, and there should have been a silence, Meyer Kappelhuist would take it upon himself to thank him, but always in a tone that said, "The law is the law and the prophets are the prophets, but prime beaver is also prime beaver, my little scholar!" It took the pleasure from Jacob's learning and the joy of the maiden from his heart. Then he would sit silent and burning, while Meyer told a great tale of Indians, slapping his hands on his knees. And in the end he was always careful to ask Jacob how many needles and pins he had sold that day; and when Jacob told him, he would smile and say very smoothly that all things had small beginnings, till the maiden herself could not keep from a little smile. Then, desperately, Jacob would rack his brain for more interesting matter. He would tell of the Wars of the Maccabees and the glory of the Temple. But even as he told them, he felt they were far away. Whereas Meyer and his accursed Indians were there, and the maiden's eyes shone at his words.

Finally he took his courage in both hands and went to Simon Ettelsohn. It took much for him to do it, for he had not been brought up to strive with men, but with words. But it seemed to him now that everywhere he went he heard of nothing but Meyer Kappelhuist and his trading with the Indians, till he thought it would drive him mad. So he went to Simon Ettelsohn in his shop.

"I am weary of this narrow trading in pins and needles,"
he said, without more words.

Simon Ettelsohn looked at him keenly; for while he was
an ambitious man, he was kindly as well. "*Nu*," he said.
"A nice little trade you have and the people like you. I myself started with less. What would you have more?"

"I would have much more," said our grandfather's grandfather stiffly. "I would have a wife and a home in this new
country. But how shall I keep a wife? On needles and
pins?"

"*Nu*, it has been done," said Simon Ettelsohn, smiling a
little. "You are a good boy, Jacob, and we take an interest
in you. Now, if it is a question of marriage, there are many
worthy maidens. Asher Levy, the baker, has a daughter. It
is true that she squints a little, but her heart is of gold." He
folded his hands and smiled.

"It is not of Asher Levy's daughter I am thinking," said
Jacob, taken aback.

Simon Ettelsohn nodded his head and his face grew
grave. "*Nu*, Jacob," he said, "I see what is in your heart.
Well, you are a good boy, Jacob, and a fine scholar. And if
it were in the old country, I am not saying. But here, I
have one daughter married to a Seixas and one to a Da
Silva. You must see that makes a difference." And he smiled
the smile of a man well-pleased with his world.

"And if I were such a one as Meyer Kappelhuist?" said
Jacob bitterly.

"Now—well, that is a little different," said Simon Ettelsohn sensibly. "For Meyer trades with the Indians. It is
true, he is a little rough. But he will die a rich man."

"I will trade with the Indians too," said Jacob, and trembled.

Simon Ettelsohn looked at him as if he had gone out of his mind. He looked at his narrow shoulders and his scholar's hands.

"Now, Jacob," he said soothingly, "do not be foolish. A scholar you are, and learned, not an Indian trader. Perhaps in a store you would do better. I can speak to Aaron Copras. And sooner or later we will find you a nice maiden. But to trade with Indians—well, that takes a different sort of man. Leave that to Meyer Kappelhuist."

"And your daughter, that rose of Sharon? Shall I leave her, too, to Meyer Kappelhuist?" cried Jacob.

Simon Ettelsohn looked uncomfortable. "*Nu,* Jacob," he said. "Well, it is not settled, of course. But—"

"I will go forth against him as David went against Goliath," said our grandfather's grandfather wildly. "I will go forth into the wilderness. And God should judge the better man!"

Then he flung his pack on the floor and strode from the shop.

Simon Ettelsohn called out after him, but he did not stop for that. Nor was it in his heart to go and seek the maiden. Instead, when he was in the street, he counted the money he had. It was not much. He had meant to buy his trading goods on credit from Simon Ettelsohn, but now he could not do that. He stood in the sunlit street of Philadelphia, like a man bereft of hope.

Nevertheless, he was stubborn—though how stubborn he did not yet know. And though he was bereft of hope, he found his feet taking him to the house of Raphael Sanchez.

Now, Raphael Sanchez could have bought and sold Simon Ettelsohn twice over. An arrogant old man he was, with fierce black eyes and a beard that was whiter than snow. He lived apart, in his big house, with his grand-daughter, and men said he was very learned, but also very disdainful, and that to him a Jew was not a Jew who did not come of the pure Sephardic strain.

Jacob had seen him, in the Congregation Mikveh Israel, and to Jacob he had looked like an eagle, and fierce as an eagle. Yet now, in his need, he found himself knocking at that man's door.

It was Raphael Sanchez himself who opened. "And what is for sale today, peddler?" he said, looking scornfully at Jacob's jacket where the pack straps had worn it.

"A scholar of the law is for sale," said Jacob in his bitterness, and he did not speak in the tongue he had learned in this country, but in Hebrew.

The old man stared at him a moment. "Now am I rebuked," he said. "For you have the tongue. Enter, my guest," and Jacob touched the scroll by the doorpost and went in.

They shared the noon meal at Raphael Sanchez's table. It was made of dark glowing mahogany, and the light sank into it as sunlight sinks into a pool. There were many precious things in that room, but Jacob had no eyes for them. When the meal was over and the blessing said, he opened his heart and spoke, and Raphael Sanchez listened, stroking his beard with one hand. When the young man had finished, he spoke.

"So, scholar," he said, though mildly, "you have crossed an ocean that you might live and not die, and yet all you see is a girl's face."

"Did not Jacob serve seven years for Rachel?" said our grandfather's grandfather.

"Twice seven, scholar," said Raphael Sanchez dryly,

"but that was in the blessed days." He stroked his beard again. "Do you know why I came to this country?" he said.

"No," said Jacob Stein.

"It was not for the trading," said Raphael Sanchez. "My house has lent money to kings. A little fish, a few furs— what are they to my house? No, it was for the promise—the promise of Penn—that this land should be a habitation and a refuge, not only for the Gentiles. Well, we know Christian promises. But so far, it has been kept. Are you spat upon in the street here, scholar of the law?"

"No," said Jacob. "They call me Jew, now and then. But the Friends, though Gentiles, are kind."

"It is not so in all countries," said Raphael Sanchez, with a terrible smile.

"No," said Jacob quietly, "it is not."

The old man nodded. "Yes, one does not forget that," he said. "The spittle wipes off the cloth, but one does not forget. One does not forget the persecutor or the persecuted. That is why they think me mad, in the Congregation Mikveh Israel, when I speak what is in my mind. For, look you"—and he pulled a map from a drawer—"here is what we know of these colonies, and here and here our people make a new beginning, in another air. But here is New France—see it?—and down the great river come the French traders and their Indians."

"Well?" said Jacob in puzzlement.

"Well?" said Raphael Sanchez. "Are you blind? I do not trust the king of France—the king before him drove out the Huguenots, and who knows what he may do? And if they hold the great rivers against us, we shall never go westward."

"We?" said Jacob in bewilderment.

"We," said Raphael Sanchez. He struck his hand on the map. "Oh, they cannot see it in Europe—not even their lords in parliament and their ministers of state," he said. "They think this is a mine, to be worked as the Spaniards worked Potosi, but it is not a mine. It is something beginning to live, and it is faceless and nameless yet. But it is our lot to be part of it—remember that in the wilderness, my young scholar of the law. You think you are going there for a girl's face, and that is well enough. But you may find something there you did not expect to find."

He paused and his eyes had a different look. "You see, it is the trader first," he said. "Always the trader, before the settled man. The Gentiles will forget that, and some of our own folk too. But one pays for the land of Canaan; one pays in blood and sweat."

Then he told Jacob what he would do for him and dismissed him, and Jacob went home to his room with his head buzzing strangely. For at times it seemed to him that the Congregation Mikveh Israel was right in thinking Raphael Sanchez half-mad. And at other times it seemed to him that the old man's words were a veil, and behind them moved and stirred some huge and unguessed shape. But chiefly he thought of the rosy cheeks of Miriam Ettelsohn.

It was with the Scotchman, McCampbell, that Jacob made his first trading journey. A strange man was Mc-Campbell, with grim features and cold blue eyes, but strong and kindly, though silent, except when he talked of the Ten Lost Tribes of Israel. For it was his contention that they were the Indians beyond the western mountains, and on this subject he would talk endlessly.

Indeed, they had much profitable conversation—Mc-Campbell quoting the doctrines of a rabbi called John Cal-

vin, and our grandfather's grandfather replying with Tal-
mud and Torah till McCampbell would almost weep that
such a honey-mouthed scholar should be destined to eternal damnation. Yet he did not treat our grandfather's
grandfather as one destined to eternal damnation, but as a
man, and he, too, spoke of cities of refuge as a man speaks
of realities, for his people had also been persecuted.

First they left the city behind them, and then the outly-
ing towns and, soon enough, they were in the wilderness. It
was very strange to Jacob Stein. At first he would wake at
night and lie awake listening, while his heart pounded, and
each rustle in the forest was the step of a wild Indian, and
each screech of an owl in the forest the whoop before the
attack. But gradually this passed. He began to notice how
silently the big man, McCampbell, moved in the woods; he
began to imitate him. He began to learn many things that
even a scholar of the law, for all his wisdom, does not know
—the girthing of a packsaddle and the making of fires, the
look of dawn in the forest and the look of evening. It was all
very new to him, and sometimes he thought he would die
of it, for his flesh weakened. Yet always he kept on.

When he saw his first Indians—in the woods, not in the
town—his knees knocked together. They were there as he
had dreamt of them in dreams, and he thought of the spirit,
Iggereth-beth-Mathlan, and her seventy-eight dancing de-
mons, for they were painted and in skins. But he could not
let his knees knock together before heathens and a Gentile,
and the first fear passed. Then he found they were grave
men, very ceremonious and silent at first, and then, when
the silence had broken, full of curiosity. They knew Mc-
Campbell, but him they did not know, and they discussed
him and his garments with the frankness of children, till

Jacob felt naked before them, and yet not afraid. One of them pointed to the bag that hung at Jacob's neck—the bag in which, for safety's sake, he carried his phylacteries —then McCampbell said something and the brown hand dropped quickly, but there was a buzz of talk.

Later on, McCampbell explained to him that they, too, wore little bags of deerskin and inside them sacred objects —and they thought, seeing his, that he must be a person of some note. It made him wonder. It made him wonder more to eat deer's meat with them, by a fire.

It was a green world and a dark one that he had fallen in—dark with the shadow of the forest, green with its green. Through it ran trails and paths that were not yet roads or highways—that did not have the dust and smell of the cities of men, but another scent, another look. These paths Jacob noted carefully, making a map, for that was one of the instructions of Raphael Sanchez. It seemed a great labor and difficult for no purpose; yet, as he had promised, so he did. And as they sank deeper and deeper into the depths of the forest, and he saw pleasant streams and wide glades, untenanted but by the deer, strange thoughts came over him. It seemed to him that the Germany he had left was very small and crowded together; it seemed to him that he had not known there was so much width to the world.

Now and then he would dream back—dream back to the quiet fields around Rettelsheim and the red-brick houses of Philadelphia, to the stuffed fish and the raisin wine, the chanting in the *chedar* and the white twisted loaves of bread under the white cloth. They would seem very close for the moment, then they would seem very far away. He was eating deer's meat in a forest and sleeping beside embers in the open night. It was so that Israel must have slept in the wilderness. He had not thought of it as so, but it was so.

Now and then he would look at his hands—they seemed tougher and very brown, as if they did not belong to him any more. Now and then he would catch a glimpse of his own face, as he drank at a stream. He had a beard, but it was not the beard of a scholar—it was wild and black. Moreover, he was dressed in skins now; it seemed strange to be dressed in skins at first, and then not strange.

Now all this time, when he went to sleep at night, he would think of Miriam Ettelsohn. But, queerly enough, the harder he tried to summon up her face in his thoughts, the vaguer it became.

He lost track of time—there was only his map and the trading and the journey. Now it seemed to him that they should surely turn back, for their packs were full. He spoke of it to McCampbell, but McCampbell shook his head. There was a light in the Scotchman's eyes now—a light that seemed strange to our grandfather's grandfather—and he would pray long at night, sometimes too loudly. So they came to the banks of the great river, brown and great, and saw it, and the countryside beyond it, like a view across Jordan. There was no end to that country—it stretched to the limits of the sky and Jacob saw it with his eyes. He was almost afraid at first, and then he was not afraid.

It was there that the strong man, McCampbell, fell sick, and there that he died and was buried. Jacob buried him on a bluff overlooking the river and faced the grave to the west. In his death sickness McCampbell raved of the Ten Lost Tribes again and swore they were just across the river and he would go to them. It took all Jacob's strength to hold him—if it had been at the beginning of the journey, he would not have had the strength. Then he turned back, for he, too, had seen a Promised Land, not for his seed only, but for nations yet to come.

Nevertheless, he was taken by the Shawnees, in a season of bitter cold, with his last horse dead. At first, when misfortune began to fall upon him, he had wept for the loss of the horses and the good beaver. But when the Shawnees took him, he no longer wept; for it seemed to him that he was no longer himself, but a man he did not know.

He was not concerned when they tied him to the stake and piled the wood around him, for it seemed to him still that it must be happening to another man. Nevertheless he prayed, as was fitting, chanting loudly; for Zion in the wilderness he prayed. He could smell the smell of the *chedar* and hear the voices that he knew—Reb Moses and Reb Nathan, and through them the curious voice of Raphael Sanchez, speaking in riddles. Then the smoke took him and he coughed. His throat was hot. He called for drink, and though they could not understand his words, all men know the sign of thirst, and they brought him a bowl, filled. He put it to his lips eagerly and drank, but the stuff in the bowl was scorching hot and burned his mouth. Very angry then was our grandfather's grandfather, and without so much as a cry he took the bowl in both hands and flung it straight in the face of the man who had brought it, scalding him. Then there was a cry and a murmur from the Shawnees and, after some moments, he felt himself unbound and knew that he lived.

It was flinging the bowl at the man while yet he stood at the stake that saved him, for there is an etiquette about such matters. One does not burn a madman, among the

Indians; and to the Shawnees Jacob's flinging the bowl proved that he was mad, for a sane man would not have done so. Or so it was explained to him later, though he was never quite sure that they had not been playing cat-and-mouse with him, to test him. Also they were much concerned by his chanting his death song in an unknown tongue and by the phylacteries that he had taken from their bag and bound upon brow and arm for his death hour, for these they thought strong medicine and uncertain. But in any case they released him, though they would not give him back his beaver, and that winter he passed in the lodges of the Shawnees, treated sometimes like a servant and sometimes like a guest, but always on the edge of peril. For he was strange to them, and they could not quite make up their minds about him, though the man with the scalded face had his own opinion, as Jacob could see.

Yet when the winter was milder and the hunting better than it had been in some seasons, it was he who got the credit for it, and the holy phylacteries also; and by the end of the winter he was talking to them of trade, though diffidently at first. Ah, our grandfather's grandfather, selig, what woes he had! And yet it was not all woe for he learned much woodcraft from the Shawnees and began to speak in their tongue.

Yet he did not trust them entirely; and when spring came and he could travel, he escaped. He was no longer a scholar then, but a hunter. He tried to think what day it was by the calendar, but he could only remember the Bee Moon. Yet when he thought of a feast he tried to keep it, and always he prayed for Zion. But when he thought of Zion, it was not as he had thought of it before—a white city set on a hill—but a great and open landscape, ready for nations. He could not have said why his thought had changed, but it had.

I shall not tell all, for who knows all? I shall not tell of the trading post he found deserted and the hundred and forty French louis in the dead man's money belt. I shall not tell of the half-grown boy, McGillvray, that he found on the fringes of a settlement—the boy who was to be his partner in the days to come—and how they traded again with the Shawnees and got much beaver. Only this remains to be told, for this is true.

It was a long time since he had even thought of Meyer Kappelhuist—the big pushing man with the red hairs on the back of his hands. But now they were turning back toward Philadelphia, he and McGillvray, their pack horses and their beaver; and as the paths began to grow familiar, old thoughts came into his mind. Moreover, he would hear now and then, in the outposts of the wilderness, of a red-haired trader. So when he met the man himself, not thirty miles from Lancaster, he was not surprised.

Now Meyer Kappelhuist had always seemed a big man to our grandfather's grandfather. But he did not seem such a big man, met in the wilderness by chance, and at that Jacob was amazed. Yet the greater surprise was Meyer Kappelhuist's, for he stared at our grandfather's grandfather long and puzzledly before he cried out, "But it's the little scholar!" and clapped his hand on his knee. Then they greeted each other civilly and Meyer Kappelhuist drank liquor, because of the meeting, but Jacob drank nothing. For all the time they were talking, he could see Meyer Kappelhuist's eyes fixed greedily upon his packs of beaver, and he did not like that. Nor did he like the looks of the three tame Indians who traveled with Meyer Kappelhuist, and, though he was a man of peace, he kept his hand on his arms, and the boy, McGillvray, did the same.

Meyer Kappelhuist was anxious that they should travel on together, but Jacob refused, for, as I say, he did not like the look in the red-haired man's eyes. So he said he was taking another road and left it at that.

"And the news you have of Simon Ettelsohn and his family—it is good, no doubt, for I know you are close to them," said Jacob, before they parted.

"Close to them?" said Meyer Kappelhuist, and he looked black as thunder. Then he laughed a forced laugh. "Oh, I see them no more," he said. "The old rascal has promised his daughter to a cousin of the Seixas, a greeny, just come over, but rich, they say. But to tell you the truth, I think we are well out of it, scholar—she was always a little too skinny for my taste." And he laughed coarsely.

"She was a rose of Sharon and a lily of the valley," said Jacob respectfully, and yet not with the pang he would have expected at such news, though it made him more determined than ever not to travel with Meyer Kappelhuist. And with that they parted and Meyer Kappelhuist went his way. Then Jacob took a fork in the trail that McGillvray knew of, and that was as well for him. For when he got to Lancaster, there was news of the killing of a trader by the Indians who traveled with him; and when Jacob asked for details, they showed him something dried on a willow hoop. Jacob looked at the thing and saw the hairs upon it were red.

"Scalped all right, but we got it back," said the frontiersman, with satisfaction. "The red devil had it on him when we caught him. Should have buried it, too, I guess, but we'd buried him already and it didn't seem feasible. Thought I might take it to Philadelphy, sometime—might make an impression on the governor. Say, if you're going there, you might—after all, that's where he come from. Be a sort of memento to his folks."

"And it might have been mine, if I had traveled with him," said Jacob. He stared at the thing again, and his heart rose against touching it. Yet it was well the city people should know what happened to men in the wilderness, and the price of blood. "Yes, I will take it," he said.

Jacob stood before the door of Raphael Sanchez, in Philadelphia. He knocked at the door with his knuckles, and the old man himself peered out at him.

"And what's your business with me, frontiersman?" said the old man, peering.

"The price of blood for a country," said Jacob Stein. He did not raise his voice, but there was a note in it that had not been there when he first knocked at Raphael Sanchez's door.

The old man stared at him soberly. "Enter, my son," he said at last, and Jacob touched the scroll by the doorpost and went in.

He walked through the halls as a man walks in a dream. At last he was sitting by the dark mahogany table. There was nothing changed in the room—he wondered greatly that nothing in it had changed.

"And what have you seen, my son?" said Raphael Sanchez.

"I have seen the land of Canaan, flowing with milk and honey," said Jacob, scholar of the law. "I have brought back grapes from Eshcol, and other things that are terrible to behold," he cried, and even as he cried he felt the sob rise in his throat. He choked it down. "Also there are

eighteen packs of prime beaver at the warehouse, and a
boy named McGillvray, a Gentile, but very trustworthy,"
he said. "The beaver is good and the boy under my protection. You will not lose on the journey. And McCampbell
died by the great river, but he had seen the land and I
think he rests well. The map is not made as I would have it,
but it shows new things. And we must trade with the
Shawnees. There are three posts to be established—I have
marked them on the map—and later, more. And beyond the
great river there is country that stretches to the end of the
world. That is where my friend McCampbell lies, with his
face turned west. But what is the use of talking? You would
not understand."

He put his head on his arms, for the room was too quiet
and peaceful, and he was very tired. Raphael Sanchez
moved around the table and touched him on the shoulder.

"Did I not say, my son, that there was more than a girl's
face to be found in the wilderness?" he said.

"A girl's face?" said Jacob. "Why, she is to be married
and, I hope, will be happy, for she was a rose of Sharon.
But what are girls' faces beside this?" and he flung something on the table. It rattled dryly on the table, like a cast
snakeskin, but the hairs upon it were red.

"It was Meyer Kappelhuist," said Jacob childishly, "and
he was a strong man. And I am not strong, but a scholar.
But I have seen what I have seen. And we must say Kad-
dish for him."

"Yes, yes," said Raphael Sanchez. "It will be done. I will
see to it."

"But you do not understand," said Jacob. "I have eaten
deer's meat in the wilderness and forgotten the month and
the year. I have been a servant to the heathen and held the

scalp of my enemy in my hand. I will never be the same man."

"Oh, you will be the same," said Sanchez. "And no worse a scholar, perhaps. But this is a new country."

"It must be for all," said Jacob. "For my friend McCampbell died also, and he was a Gentile."

"Let us hope," said Raphael Sanchez, and touched him again upon the shoulder. Then Jacob lifted his head and he saw that the light had declined and the evening was upon them. And even as he looked, Raphael Sanchez's granddaughter came in to light the candles for Sabbath. And Jacob looked upon her, and she was a dove, with dove's eyes.

THE LAST MAN ALIVE

CONRAD RICHTER

It's just a relic today, a huge old box, plain and ugly as sin, with a heavy and unwieldy lid. The date, 1762, when probably it was made, is carved crudely in the dark-stained pine. Those who pass it in the museum scarcely give it a glance. Of what use is such an ancient and monstrous thing in this modern world? they think. For never in those early times did folks have such terrible problems to solve as today.

But if you wait till the guard has wandered into another room, you may, if you are strong enough, lift the heavy lid. And in the breath of vanished old quilts and early American life rising from the grain of wood you may catch the faint scent of hickory smoke and May apples that clung around the dress of Jess Galloway, the bound girl, as she stood that day of the mid-Revolution in the tiny settlement of Fisher Valley and faced what the future held for them all.

Oh, she knew what awful thing was wrong with the world, and had known it for some time. Men in a hurry had been stopping off in the settlement on their way south. What they said was told only to the men behind closed doors, but you could leave it to the women to find out. And when they had, they wished they hadn't, for this wasn't just an Indian scare. No, this was extinction, the end of the world for Central and Northern Pennsylvania, and perhaps much farther. The enemy was leading the savage to burn, scalp, and exterminate. In all this great empire of forest, no white men or women were to be left alive.

Ever since spring, settler folk had been driven out, but now, with the terrible news from the Wyoming Valley of Pennsylvania, those still left were a clearing out their own selves. That was a sight to see, men, women, and young ones in boats, arks, canoes, rafts—anything that would float, even hog troughs—a running down the Susquehanna! Most of their farm and household stuff had to be left behind. And this was only the West Branch. It was the same on the North Branch. Where did all the displaced settler folks come from? Jess wondered, for these were just the lucky ones that got away. Behind them in clearings for many a mile folks lay with woods flies a buzzing at their hacked heads and at the brains of their littlest ones busted against trees.

But do you reckon the men in Fisher Valley would go? No, not them. They said the Dunkards on the other side of Third Gap in Limestone Valley weren't going at all, and Fisher Valley would wait till its crops were harvested. Even then it would be hard enough to give up the good black land they had cleared and the log buildings they had raised. Their flax they would have to leave unpulled, and their corn stand small and green in the field. But their wheat and rye they could reap, thresh, sack, and tote along. It would give them bread this coming winter wherever they might be.

Now today the last of the wheat was being flailed, and tomorrow they would go. Hardly could Jess believe that this was their last day in the valley. Seldom had she seen a seemlier one. The air from the English Lakes blew clear and crystal over Shade Mountain. The July sun lay golden on the long, ragged wheat stubble. Blue dinner smoke rose from the small cluster of clay chimneys, and the gray walls of the settlement looked as soft and homelike as guinea fowl.

But where was Ashael? All morning Jess had asked this of herself. Here it was the last day and no sight of the stern young Amishman who last spring had asked the elder to marry them. The elder could have done it, too, for it was given him to baptize and marry as well as preach. But he wouldn't set Jess free till her contract was up. You might think Ashael would get mad, so straight and small and doughty he stood, with a blue eye like ice in his sightly face framed by his red hair and beard. But the Amish were men of God, and more patient than this one looked. All he said was he would wait, and went back to his bachelor improvement over Shade Mountain.

This morning, threshing on the barn floor, Jess kept going to the door. But never did she get a sight of his clean black suit, fastened with hooks and eyes, and his blacker hat with the broad brim.

"If it's Ashael you look for, you needn't," the elder told her at last. "He's not coming."

The bound girl felt the flail strike against her heart. "Didn't you send him word?" she cried.

"Oh, he's plenty word. Not for anything but God would he leave his place, he said. You ought to remember how stubborn he is. Not a penny would he pay to buy off your contract. Not even to marry you."

"Why should he?" Jess stuck up for him. "He's just starting out, and poor."

"Not so poor. He has the Great Chest from the old country. But he wouldn't part with it."

"What would be the use? He can wait two years and get me for nothing."

"Yes, if you stay single for him. But how does he know some other man won't come along and buy you off from me? You're big and strong and a good worker. Some even say you're good to look at. Women don't grow on every bush in this country."

"Ashael don't need to worry. I'll wait for him," Jess said stolidly.

Just the same, hardly could she eat her early noon dinner. In the middle of it a Tioga man with long hair and a boy on the saddle in front of him rode out of the woods shouting terrible words. He halted by the elder's house and called that Dunkardtown in Limestone Valley had been

burned. All were wiped out. Wasn't there some saved, Jake
Bender asked. Not a Dunkard lifted his hand or complained, the stranger said, for that was against their belief.
"It's God's will," was all they said as the tomahawk fell on
themselves and their families. Of the whole settlement, only
this boy he found hiding in the woods was left to tell him
what happened.

Everybody in little Fisher Valley had crowded to hear
and sicken, everybody save Jess. All she could think of was
Ashael alone over in his valley. None saw her, except it
might be Mary, as she put the house between her and the
people. By the run, her feet fell on the Indian path across
the mountain.

Many a time when she went for the cows or on a Sabbath
walk had she thought of her marriage day when she would
take this path to Ashael's valley. First the path led through
a wide hollow of noble pines and hemlocks. Even in winter
the snow looked dark in here. Beyond was the spring where
the great velvet bird's-foot violet and yellow lady's-slipper
grew. Oh, this path would be a mortal sweet place to walk
on your marriage day, but today she saw feathers in every
bush and a spear in every sapling.

So thick stood the forest on the north side she could get
no look at the valley below. Not till she reached the bottom,
had waded Ashael's creek, and climbed around the limestone outcrop did she come out in the clearing. There stood
the peaceful scene like always. Ashael's log cabin, his
round-log barn, his stumpy fields in wheat, grass, and corn,
with a patch of potatoes by the house. From the woods
came the lazy tank-tank-tank of a cowbell. The wheat
stood uncut, for the season came a little later over here. In
the hayfield loading his cart was Ashael.

His horse, lonesome over here in this valley, gave a little whinny at the sight of Jess. Until then, Ashael didn't see her. That was Ashael all over. The savages could crawl within a dozen yards of him and never would he believe they were there. He looked for good, not for evil. But he was the man for her, Jess told herself, seeing him again standing there by his cart so straight and doughty for such a little fellow, and mighty brave to be living by himself over here in the wilderness.

His face hardly changed as she told him about Dunkard-town. His eyes kept looking around his little farm in the clearing. She hardly believed that he heard her. His strong cheeks kept warding off the bad words, so that it seemed even to Jess what she said couldn't be. The hay smelled tame and sweet like always over here in this peaceful valley. Wheat stood gold as a sovereign on the stalk. A bird sang mighty pretty in the forest, and over them stood the mountain like a sentry on guard. Only the ugly recollection of what the Tioga man had said kept coming back to plague her.

"Don't look at your crops, Ashael!" she begged him. "Just go before it's too late!"

"Run off, you mean?" He looked at her sharply. "Where can you go from the hand of the Lord? He can strike you down in Lancaster town as easy as up here."

"He kin," Jess agreed. "But most likely He won't want to. Now I can't say that much for the Injuns."

"No red man would do me harm," Ashael promised. "Not a one ever left my door without something to eat or a place to sleep."

"That's what the Dunkards used to say, and look what happened to them!"

"It was the Lord's will," he said, very low, but Jess heard him.

"The Lord had nothin' to do with it," she declared warmly. "The Dunkards just wouldn't stand up and defend themselves."

"It's in our Bible. If your adversary strike you, turn the other cheek."

"You don't always git a chance to do that with an Injun," Jess observed. "Once his tomahawk hits you, you're a gone Josie. You got to hit him first."

"Our people," Ashael said, "don't take up arms against anybody."

"Wouldn't you lift a hand to save your own self . . . or me?"

"No, for to lose your life is to save it."

Jess looked at him. "Then it's true what Elder Kring said about you."

"What did he say?"

"That you were stubborn as a mule."

"I'm glad if I'm stubborn in my belief."

"Well, if you want to be stubborn, I kin too," she told him. "It says in the Bible it's not good for man to be alone. And if you won't come with us, I'm a goin' to stay up here with you."

The first alarm crossed the Amishman's face. "No, that you can't do."

"Why can't I? Who'll stop me?"

"I will," Ashael promised. "Never will I live with a woman in sin!"

"It would be only for a year or two," Jess explained. "When a parson comes through, we kin be married. If none comes, we could go down the river sometime . . . once our young ones are old enough."

"That's enough!" Ashael cried, and his face was dark with anger. "Till your time is up, you belong to the elder! If you won't go back yourself, I'll have to take you!"

Jess's mouth got a peculiar ropy look, and if Ashael had known her better, he might have taken warning. But at that moment rumbling sounds rolled along the mountains, as of distant thunder.

"You ought to git your hay in first, Ashael," she said mildly. "I kin help you. Then you kin send me over."

"How do I know," he asked sternly, "that a girl who would live in sin will keep her word?"

"You're a man," Jess said, still meek as Moses. "And if I wouldn't, you could make me."

"Yes, well," Ashael agreed. "If you want to help a little, Jess, I won't say no. Afterwards, I'll walk with you over the mountain. I meant to go over anyway and give everybody good-by."

The rest of the day, scarcely speaking, they worked in the hayfield. Jess raked the hay into piles and stood on the cart to stamp down the fork loads from Ashael. Sometimes she took the fork her own self and swung up as heavy loads as he. She believed she could lift still heavier, but never would she shame Ashael in his own field. It took longer than they reckoned. When they finished, the sun was already down behind North Mountain. The valley felt cooler in shadow. But where was the storm whose thunder they had heard? The sky still hung without a cloud and blue as a gentian.

"Hadn't we better milk before we go?" Jess asked, still

mild. And when the milking was done: "Ashael, I'm a mite hungry. I guess it's from the hay and crossing the mountain. If you feed every savage that comes this way, maybe you could spare me a bite of supper. It wouldn't hurt you to eat either."

He gave her a searching look, but did not refuse. Sitting there at the hewn table in Ashael's cabin, with Ashael's own bread and milk between them, with his fireplace on one side, his gun, that must be used only for game, in the corner behind the door, his bed on the floor, and near it the long chest that came from the old country, Jess felt almost like already she was Ashael's wife and mistress of his house and lands. Never, she told herself, would she give him up now. First she would put him off till tomorrow. Then the elder and the Fisher Valley folks would be gone.

So long did she keep sitting at the table after Ashael finished that he grew uneasy and restless. He got up and put away all save her bowl and spoon. Now with impatience, he watched her make what little she had left last a long time. Daylight faded from the cabin, so that already it seemed dark in here.

"I have seen many eat, but never a bird like you," he told her at last. "How do you get any work done?"

"I kin work with any woman!" Jess shot at him. "Or with a man either!"

"Then let's see how good you climb the mountain," he said, "or it will be dark on us before we get started."

She pushed back her bowl and spoon. "It's no use, Ashael," she said. "I'm not a goin' off without you."

She was not prepared for the terrible look that came on his face. "So the word of a girl that would live in sin is not worth anything after all?" he lashed her.

"I never said I'd go . . . only that you could make me," Jess reminded.

"So I could . . . if I wanted to," he rebuked her.

For a minute they faced each other, Jess with her black hair and slate-gray eyes, and Ashael with his red beard and hair and his eyes blue as limestone. He stood so straight and righteous for such a little fellow. Oh, he had muscles you could never pinch. He could give her a tussle, if he wanted to. But in her heart Jess knew that never could he throw her and drag her out. No, rather she could swing him off the floor and set him where she wanted.

"Only my belief stops me," he said, bleak as a plowed field in winter. "You needn't worry. I won't lift my hands against you any more than against an Indian."

He went to his long chest and began lifting out what lay inside. He made all into two piles and tied them up in the blankets from his bed. Then he went for the door.

"Where are you goin', Ashael?" she asked.

"Not with you, woman," he said. "If you won't go from here, then you can stay and I will go. The Indians can't drive me off. Only one like you can. If you come after me, I'll leave where I am and go up to Dunkardtown."

"Dunkardtown is burnt, Ashael."

"Not the land. A new house and barn I can build for myself."

Quietly she sat at the table. Presently she could hear him out at the barn, hitching up and throwing his farm things in the cart. He drove to the door and started to carry out his packs and kettles.

"You needn't do that, Ashael," she said, getting up. "I only reckoned to stay and help you with your work and cook your meals and sew your clothes. But I won't run you off your own place. If you won't stay, then I'll go my own self."

"You said that before."

"I'll go for sure now," she said. "Good-by, Ashael."

"Wait! I want to go along and see that you do what you say!" he said sternly.

"You needn't. I gave my word now."

"I'll go just the same," he told her. "You could hide in the woods and come back tonight or tomorrow. It has neither bar nor lock on my door."

Well, it was all over, Jess told herself, as they tramped up the mountain. Likely this was the last time that ever she would see him or cross Shade Mountain. It was pitch dark when they reached the summit. The moon would soon be up, Ashael said, and then they could see, once they got out of the timber.

"You're sure they didn't leave this morning already?" he asked of a sudden, when they were halfway down.

Oh, she knew what made his suspicion. She had noticed it herself—the smell of smoke; not the good homelike scent of chimney smoke, but the rank stench of burning household logs, chinking, and rubbish. It grew stronger as they went by the dark spring, through the black pines and hemlocks and by the unseen swamp, where the cows liked to get away from the flies. Then suddenly they came out of the woods and saw in the darkness before them great red eyes winking at them from where the settlement ought to be.

"Ashael, don't go any farther!" she warned him.

Ashael had stopped, but only for a moment. "I'm not scared," he told her. "Nobody will hurt an Amishman. But you better stay back. I can't answer for you."

It was true, Ashael feared nothing, she told herself, as he went on, with her following close behind. Her eyes could barely make out the path in the meadow they followed. Halfway across, Ashael stumbled over something, and she thought she heard him take the Lord's name under his breath. When she reached down, her hand froze. Here in the path she could feel a dress and apron she thought she knew, but the body diked out in them lay stiff and cold. "Ashael!" she cried, stifling a scream. "It's Mary!"

Ashael stood by with a man's clumsy sympathy. She could not see his face, but he did not take off his broad-brim hat. "God's will be done," he muttered in the dialect.

Huddled there above the silent body of her friend, Jess waited while the story of this shocking thing worked like a deadly poison through her mind. The savages must have struck that afternoon not long after she had gone, and that had been the rattle of distant thunder that she and Ashael had heard. Likely Mary had run for the mountain, too, and here they had overtaken her. In her mind's eye Jess could see a savage with his uplifted tomahawk cutting her down.

For a while longer she and Ashael stood there, listening, watching. Not a shadow moved across the dying red beds of coals. No sound rose save the hoot of some big-eared owl up the valley. Where the settlement had stood and flourished with human life and household comforts, and with shelter and feed for the stork, now all was death and desolation.

When he started on, she came after. She remembered the saying of Jake Bender that seldom the savages attack at night. No, they preferred to do their dirty work in the day-time and camp by evening in some hidden spot far from their bloody deeds. Just the same, she would have felt better with Ashael's gun in her hands. When they reached the ashes of the elder's barn, no rifle cracked or arrow sang, though they stood plain targets against the scarlet-orange embers. As they stayed on there, the moon came up, lately full, bulging a little on one side, as if misshapen with the evil of the night. Rather she would have had it down, for now they had to put their eyes on what there was to see.

One by one, they accounted for all of the settlement save three. Tilly Fegley they found lying on her face, scalped; and Mordecai with his wounded head in the spring that still flowed a little red, Jess fancied. Jake Bender was a mutilated sight and the reason plain to see, for his gun, with the barrel bent nearly double, lay by the ashes of his house. His wife and old mother were behind the wall of the barn, and Sairy lay in the garden, her sunbonnet hanging on a scorched bush of little dark-brown blooms that the Pennsylvania Dutch call shrubs. The Tioga man and the boy on the front of his saddle must have gone before the attack. Not a trace of them could be found, or of the two small Fegley boys. Likely they were taken prisoner, for young whites make as good Indians as red ones. But where was the elder?

Then, as they came to the walnut by the run, a figure with gory head sat up and asked for a drink of water. He was a fearful sight to see, like somebody rising from the grave. His eyes already had the glaze of death, and when Jess ran with water in a broken pot, he had lain back again and barely could he swallow.

"Where are the others?" he whispered.

"They are here," Jess told him.

"Gone, all gone," he moaned.

"All save the Fegley young ones," Ashael said.

"And they are worse than dead," Jess added bitterly.

"Well, I am not long for this world either," the elder said, very low.

"You'll be better by morning, perhaps," Ashael promised.

"Don't fool yourself, Ashael," the elder whispered hoarsely. "Don't wait too long, like we did."

Ashael didn't say anything.

The elder went on. "One time you asked for Jess. Now I give her to you. She's no good to me any more."

Jess saw Ashael flinch.

"She must go down the river, elder," he said. "We are not married."

The elder lay a while breathing heavily, his pale eyes fixed on one and then on the other. "You want him in marriage, Jess?"

She turned slowly and looked at Ashael. "If he's a willin'," she said.

Together, she and Ashael waited. The elder lay for a while with closed eyes. They did not know if he was dead or dying, but then he looked at them.

"In the name of the Father, the Son, and the Holy Ghost!" he began in a voice so strong it startled them. "We are gathered together for the purpose of holy matrimony—"

That was the strangest wedding Jess Galloway ever knew, with never a house or room to be married in, with nothing but the night air to stand in, with the holy words said by a preacher cut down like a tree on the ground, and with the moon for light, while around them still glowed the evil embers. One time the voice of the dying elder rang out like that of God Himself, and then again it grew so faint that Jess had to bend her head to listen, for never would she miss hearing the words of her own marrying. But the worst was that Mary and Sairy couldn't be with her at her wedding.

She was Ashael's lawful wife now, she told herself when it was over. It put iron in her as she went around with him fetching the bodies in to be buried in the elder's root cellar. Never could they dig a separate grave for each this night. Here they could lay them all side by side, with the oldest at one end and the youngest at the other. Many times Jess went over their order in her mind, so she could tell where each lay. They had no box, but Ashael spread over them some bedclothes stiff with blood that had missed the fire. Then Ashael, with the pick, and Jess, with the shovel, caved in the earthen roof of the root cellar and covered them over with the dark, rich soil. Not till they were done did Jess come on freshly cut grass and leaves covering a spot of ground. When they bared it, they found a new grave. Ashael said it was an Indian grave, and if they dug, likely they would find the savages accounted for by Jake Bender.

It was late, and the bulging moon half gone across the sky, when they started back to their place in Ashael's valley. Rather would Jess have gone for the river, had Ashael been willing, but she was a married woman now, and where her man went she would have to follow. Oh, never, when she thought ahead of marrying Ashael someday, did she expect such a sober wedding journey as this over Shade Mountain in the dead of night, with the lonesome feeling that in this vast region they were the only white people left alive.

Her first word she spoke when they came to the summit. "Ashael, do you reckon you could do something for me and count it a weddin' present?"

"If I can, Jess, I'll do it," Ashael promised. Never had his voice sounded kinder.

"Will you put a bar on the door tonight when we git home?"

He was silent a while, and she knew she had displeased him. "I'll do it, like I said, if you want me," he agreed. "But it can do no good. Those who come by my house are always welcome, and I'd have to open the door anyhow."

Jess felt thunderstruck. "You mean you'd open to those red devils?"

"Their skins are red, but they have souls like we do," Ashael reproved her.

"Yes, souls black as the pots of hell!" Jess told him. "They'll never come in my house!"

"Then I'll have to go outside and talk to them."

"After what you saw tonight?"

"They did a bad thing, and I don't stand up for it," Ashael said. "But 'vengeance is mine; I will repay, saith the Lord.' Anyway, they would never do it to me."

"But what if they did?" Jess demanded.

"Then it would be God's will," Ashael said humbly.

Jess's face in the darkness was bitter. In her heart she prayed that Ashael's barn and house might be burned down when they got there. It would mean that the savages had come and gone. If the house and barn stood, it meant it was still to be. Oh, never for a minute did she expect that they would be overlooked. The savages knew every white place north of the mountains. Not an improvement but was marked in their minds for destruction.

Her prayer was not answered. When they came up the cart path, around the shale bank, and into the clearing,

there stood the house and barn in the moonlight exactly
as they had left them. The ax raised up undisturbed from
the chopping block. From the barn came Gruzel's whinny,
and from the woods the lazy tank-tank of Star's bell. The
moon itself hung peaceful far up the valley, throwing long
shadows over the fields. Only the black stumps made her
think of savages a hiding in the wheat. She picked up the
ax from the chopping block and took it in with her. Inside
the cabin, once they had lit a fire of hickory bark for light,
all was tranquil and untouched.

Was it possible she had been wrong? she asked herself.
Could it be that those red heathen would not bother
Ashael, knowing his ways for peace? Then she forgot her
fears, for this was her wedding night. . . .

It was getting daylight when she awoke. Now what had
awakened her, she wondered. Then she heard it again—
an anxious whinny from the barn. Jess got up swiftly and
went to the open window. A morning fog covered the valley, but it was not heavy enough to keep her from seeing
a file of three figures coming, silent as the mist itself, from
the woods. Almost she gave a cry of joy, for the first looked
like a woman in a red-check gown. With a flash of warm
feeling, it came to her that no longer was she the only
white woman in these lonesome woods. Today she would
have another of her kind for company. Then the joy died
in her throat as she saw that the figure carried a rifle, like
the others, and that all three had the same tufted and half-
shaven heads. Suddenly she knew, with a wave of horror,
where she had seen red checks like that before—in a table-
cloth from some Pennsylvania Dutch settler's house, now
likely in ashes and its mistress murdered close by.

"Ashael!" she tried to rouse him. As the file of men came

closer, her eyes tried to make out what beside rifles they carried. Furry objects, they looked like, some short, some long and flowing, some black, brown, and fair as tow. Now she recognized them for what they were—scalps stretched over hoops to dry, and perhaps the freshest was the long chestnut hair of Mary Bender.

"Ashael!" she begged, and touched him, but his breathing never changed from the long, deep snores that all night had seemed to suck up the air around her, so there was none left for her to breathe. Oh, she knew men were heavier sleepers than women. Mary used to say that her father would sleep through a thunder-and-lightning storm. But this man of hers must be the master sleeper of the lot. Or else his work of yesterday, the strain last evening, and, on top of that, his wedding night, had been too much for him. In his red frame of beard, his sleeping face looked like a saint's, but one that even in his dreams knew his own will and would suffer none to change it.

She looked around. The great dower chest still stood open, its lid back against the wall as Ashael had left it last evening. She bent down and slipped her strong young arms under his back and knees. The rhythm of his breathing changed for a moment. Surely now he must get awake. Then, after a lick, his snores rang out stronger than ever, as if to drown out this interference. She lifted him quickly over inside. His knees had to stick up. His snoring had stopped now. She set a chip on the chest's edge for air and closed the lid. Then her fingers fastened the iron catch with the peg.

Now, God forgive her, but there Ashael would have to stay. In her bare feet she went to the door and braced it shut with a puncheon. As she straightened she saw a curious-looking stick moving beyond the window. It pushed higher and closer to the sill. Then she knew it for a bruised and splintered ramrod sticking out from its thimbles. A greasy rifle barrel and painted face followed, both turning this way and that, trying to find the Amishman in his bed.

Jess's hands were slowly fixed on Ashael's gun standing by her in the door corner. An ancient and heavy piece, the fore stock had been fastened to the barrel with bands of tow. Whether it was loaded or not, Jess did not know, only that Ashael's other gear he kept in working order. This gun might never be used save on game, but if she knew Ashael, it would be primed and ready. She cocked the hammer. At the click, the savage looked up and saw her in the dimness. Before he could turn his rifle, she drew a bead on that paint-streaked face and pressed the rusty old trigger.

The roar echoed through the cabin. Then, as the sound kept on, Jess realized it wasn't the shot any more, but a violent pounding inside the chest.

"Jess!" Ashael shouted. "Let me out!"

She paid him no attention. The savage was gone from the window, but now she heard them at the door. Oh, that was the savage way—to draw a white man's fire and then get at him with the tomahawk before he had time to reload. Jess threw down Ashael's gun, for it was no use to her now, and set her stout body against the door, with the ax beside her.

"Jess, live you yet?" Ashael called. "Let me free!"

"I live yet, Ashael, but I can't let you free!"

"Woman, open this chest!" he ordered in anger.

Oh, if Ashael wasn't a godly person, if only he had been one to quarrel and fight, like Jake Bender, she couldn't have opened the lid quick enough. If ever she needed a man by her side, she needed him now. But not a lover of peace to open the door, hold out his hands, and then all he could say was, "God's will," when a bullet fetched him down. Rather have him stay where he was. That's why she had put him there. And yet, how could she hold the door herself against three? Already the puncheon was beginning to slip in the earthen floor. She could hear the savages' fearful yells of exultation as they felt the door give. In violent jerks and shovings, they pressed it far enough for one with his hatchet to worm himself a little way through, and another to put his head after.

With her strong foot and thigh wedged against the door, Jess held them there. Ashael's ax hung clenched in her long, powerful fingers. Now her face grew cruel and the memory of what pitiful things she had seen last night steeled her arms and heart. Sucking in her breath, she raised the heavy bit.

"That's for Mary!" she cried, when she fetched it down. "And that's for Sairy!" she cried louder, as she struck again and kept on till both lay like butchered bullocks between hewn door and log jamb. Then, taking a fresh hold, she waited for the third. But although she stood there a long time, none came. She opened the door a little wider. The mist had thinned. After a while the sun rose over Shade Mountain. The clearing looked calm and peaceful in the light. She could hear the sound of water running over stones in Ashael's creek. Over and over again came the mortal sweet song of the wood robin.

Not till then did she think of the window. It flashed through her mind that the other savage could have reloaded and shot her in the back while she stood there. But when she went to the window, she saw him lying on the ground.

The loud rattling of the chest roused her. Well, she had done what she could. She guessed she must let Ashael out now. Much rather she wouldn't, for it would take a braver body to stand up to Ashael than to the savages. Making a sober face, she pulled out the peg and laid back the lid. She knew then she wasn't wrong, for his face was like the avenging angel's when he came out. Not a word did he say to her, even after he saw the savages at the door. In silence he took the gun and ax, and carried them out to the barn. When he returned, it was with the shovel and grubbing hoe.

Long before he came in, she had breakfast ready, and he ate his fill, but not a word could she get out of him. His face was grim as stone. Oh, she had time now to think over what she had done to him. She had lifted her hands in arms against those who came to his house. She had saved him, but she had disgraced him too. More than once had she heard of a Swiss or Dutch wife who bedeviled her man till he made a vow never to speak to her again. Not for a minute had she dreamed she would do such a thing to Ashael. She should have known better. Never need she expect him to open his mouth to her again.

That's the way it worked out. Corn ripened, was cut, and husked. Snow fell and melted. Ice formed on the gats. Snow fell again, and this time it laid. Now, wasn't it too bad? They were two that had been spared from the heathen, maybe the only two for a hundred miles, and here they had to live together like dumb brutes in the stall! When he sat with her at their table, it was like he had no tongue. Even

THE LAST MAN ALIVE

his prayers to his Maker were dumb. Only his lips moved.

Well, if he would say no word, neither would she, not even about the babe she carried. When the pains came on her one night in April, never did she let on. She got his breakfast like usual, though hardly could she wait to get rid of him from the house. The young one gave her a hard tussle before it was born. More than once that morning she would like to have called to Ashael for help, but she set her jaws tight. If he could take care of his business without talking, so could she. More than once she had helped with birthing. Now she tended to herself, crawling to the fire on her hands and knees for warm water to wash the babe, to smooth it down afterward with melted coon tallow, and for the child's long flannel gown she had long since sewed with Ashael's coarse thread and needle.

Back in her floor bed, Jess lay with her babe close by her. Well, Ashael could hold his tongue from this hour if he wanted. She had a man now she could talk to and listen to. Already he was telling her things at the top of his Tom Thumb lungs. If Ashael wasn't plowing in the far field, he couldn't help but hear him.

Toward noon, when the babe slept, she was startled to hear somebody talking. It must be Ashael talking to the horse, she reckoned. Then she heard voices she had never heard before—white men's voices. They sounded from the barn. After a while she could tell they were coming toward the house, for it was noon and time for dinner.

Not soon would she forget how strange and shy she felt when the soldier stepped into the cabin. Why, he was the first human being, besides Ashael and the baby, she had laid eyes on since early last summer! Behind him came another. Both carried muskets.

"You didn't say you had a baby!" the first one called out.

Jess saw Ashael reach out his head at that. Oh, never a word did he say, but a look spread on his face that Jess never saw before and hardly ever after. He stood for a shake not knowing what to do, and this his own house and household goods. Then he came over to the bed, and Jess saw him watching the little old puckered red face sticking from the bedclothes beside her.

"It's a girl or boy, Jess?" he asked very low.

"It's a boy."

"You all right?"

"I'm real good."

"Can I get you anything?"

"No, but I reckon you'll have to git your own dinner," she told him.

That's all he said and that's all she said, but never would Jess have believed the good feeling that ran over her. Ashael had talked to her. Nerve strings she never reckoned she had in her body let go. The cabin took on a different look, like it had the first time she laid eyes on it. Through the window she could see the bright sunshine on the red flowers of the maples. Down in the gats peepers were calling.

Ashael got dinner, with the two soldiers helping. All the time they swapped news. Their talk sounded sweet as music in Jess's ear.

"We never expected to find somebody living up here," the first soldier said. "I still can't get it through my head. How was it the Indians didn't get you?"

Ashael thought a minute. He looked over at Jess, and his face was sober as a dominie's on Sunday. "It was the will of God," he said shortly.

CAP GITCHIE'S ROOSTER

JIM KJELGAARD

Cap Gitchie came out of the Kentucky woods three miles ahead of the posse that was chasing him. As he approached the huts, cabins, and houses that sheltered the inhabitants of Louisville, he slowed down to a leisurely walk and strolled down to take a look at the river. The sun had not yet climbed over the eastern horizon, and a fine mist hovered over the famous falls, where the Ohio River dropped twenty-two feet in two miles. But at this flood season no white water boiled and thundered over the cataract. Disappointed, Cap walked down to Bear Grass Creek, where the keel and flatboats were tied—fourteen feet wide by fifty long—a black-and-white dog rose from the coil of rope where it had been sleeping, and growled at him. The dog's ruff bristled, and it began to bark in a loud and irritating voice.

Cap Gitchie drew back his right foot, the one that had kicked many a clamoring dog from his path, and experimentally snapped it forward. A wide grin split his mouth and raised the ends of his straggling mustache. He had traveled something over a hundred miles in two days, and there had not been much time for sleeping or resting. But there was enough power left in his foot to take care of any flatboat cur. Cap shifted the long rifle, a bare ten inches shorter than his own six feet three, from his right hand to his left. The movement woke up the rooster on his shoulder.

It was a small rooster that could not have weighed more than four or four and a half pounds. But its sweeping length, that started in a slim, snakelike, combless head and ended in a long, gracefully curved sickle of tail feathers, lent an impression of much greater size. The rooster's legs were long and trim, and his spurs were sharp. But it was his fierce, intelligent eyes that set him apart from the ordinary rooster found prowling about the barns and manure piles of the settlers along the Ohio. They were the eyes of a thoroughbred gamecock.

When the rooster came awake it flapped its wings. Standing erect on its owner's shoulder, it sent its challenging crow echoing over the river. From one of the moored flatboats another rooster answered. The red cock preened itself, turning its head from side to side and blinking in the

half-light of early morning, while it sought the exact source
from which its invitation to battle had been accepted. It
clucked throatily and made ready to crow again. Cap
Gitchie reached up with his right hand, and twined his
fingers softly about the red rooster's throat.

"Suppose," he suggested, "that you shut up. Ain't you
got me in enough trouble already?" And as though suddenly remembering, he glanced back at the dark forest out
of which he had come.

It was just about a year and a half ago that he had landed
in America, at Baltimore. His arrival had not been wholly
orthodox. But, on the other hand, it hadn't been exactly
jumping ship, either, because to go back on the *St. John*
would only have meant to be clapped in irons while the
vessel sailed back to England. Captain Marritt, of the *St.
John*, was a hard driver of men. But it had been a mistake
when he chose, after the anchorage in Chesapeake Bay, to
use his lash on Cap Gitchie. After the fight started, Captain
Marritt had even used a belaying pin. But he hadn't used
it well enough, and he had been lying on the deck in an
undetermined state of disrepair when Cap Gitchie took a
hasty departure.

Ashore, Cap had seen the red rooster scratching about
a refuse heap on the water front. A man had to eat, and
chicken was mighty tasty. Snatching up the rooster, Cap
had resumed his journey. Ten miles out of Baltimore, with
every intention of wringing its neck, he had taken the red
rooster from his shirt and had had his hand soundly pecked.
A man just couldn't eat a spunky rooster like that, especially
after it climbed to his shoulder and seemed entirely content
to ride there. He was in a strange land, where a man needed
a good friend, and the rooster had amply proven his friend-

ship in Pittsburgh, where, in less than a minute, he had whipped to a standstill the gray rooster that a Pittsburgh merchant brought against him. So doing, he had also enriched Cap's purse by two pounds five shillings. But after he had defeated the town's champion, it was impossible to get any more fights in Pittsburgh—for the rooster.

By slow stages, sleeping where night overtook him if he happened to be in wild country, and sleeping between blankets when he came across an inn, Cap and his rooster had fought their way down the Ohio. Two of a kind, they had accepted and defeated all comers. But it was not until they had reached Limestone, a raw Ohio River frontier town, that they had met with real trouble. Cap had wagered all the money he had picked up since Baltimore— twenty-five pounds—that his red rooster was better than Limestone's best blue cock. And it had been.

But how was he, Cap Gitchie, to know that Limestoners were hard losers, or that, without settling their bets, they'd threaten him with a long rifle and order him to leave town? And how was he to know that after he'd taken the rifle away from the man who held it, and collected his winnings, he'd have to race into the southern forest with a posse of Limestoners on his heels? A man couldn't guess such things in advance. All he could do was run—fast.

The rooster crowed again, flapped his wings, and a second time sent his ringing crow rolling over the assembled keel and flatboats. There was a sudden motion on a keelboat anchored to some willows a bare twenty feet from where Cap was standing. A brisk little man dressed in a suit of almost-white woolen underwear emerged from the cabin and blinked his eyes sleepily. A fringe of gray hair clung precariously to the sides of his otherwise bald head, and his chin was adorned with a matted beard that resembled nothing so much as a handful of gray-colored straw.

"Now who might ye be?" he demanded snappishly.

Cap Gitchie folded his long arms, cradling the rifle in the crook of his right elbow. "Might be George Washington, or the king of France. But I ain't."

"Where ye from?"

"From every place but here, and I'll soon be from here."

The little man stamped to the bow of his keelboat, and surveyed Cap from top to toe. "How old are ye, mister?"

"Old enough"—Cap was twenty-four— "to mind my own business."

The little man suddenly smiled. "Ye talk like a boatman. Moreover, ye talk like a keelboatman. Ever been to New Orleans?"

"Now what would I be doin' in New Orleans?"

"Talkative cuss, ain't ye?" the bearded man snapped. "How should I know what ye'd be doin' there? All I want to know is do ye want to go? If ye do, I can use another boatman—fifteen dollars and found for the trip. If so be ye can ever make up yer mind, come and see me—Abijah Ezekiel Primpton Crabbe, owner and cap'n of the *River Belle*, cargoes to and from New Orleans, and tradin' done to order."

Cap Gitchie wandered back into Louisville, and the rooster flew from his shoulder to scratch about in a patch of green grass. He industriously swallowed bugs and worms, while Cap stood gazing at an inn, thinking of his own breakfast. It was too early for the inn to open, but he was hungry. A kick on the door might awaken the proprietor, and Cap was ready to deliver that kick when motion back at the edge of the forest caught his eye. Eight tall buck-

skinned men broke out of the woods, and with long rifles
held ready marched grimly into town.

Cap snatched up the rooster and raced toward the river.
He paused momentarily before the *River Belle*, then leaped
from the bank and landed on the deck. Almost instantly
he was confronted by Abijah Crabbe and a big flintlock
pistol. Cap smiled pleasantly.

"I decided to take your offer," he said, "if my rooster gets
passage and found, too."

"That'll cost ye a dollar," Abijah Crabbe said.

"And we'll have to get off right away."

The little man glanced toward the shore. He'd had previous experience with men who suddenly made up their
minds to go keelboating in a hurry. "That'll be four dollars
extry," he snapped.

Cap sighed dolefully. "A third of my wages gone, and we
ain't even started yet. Let's move."

Cap Gitchie took his place at one of the two starboard
oars and timed his stroke to that of the blithe and carefree
Irishman ahead of him. Directly across, on the other side of
the same seat, sat a lanky Kentuckian with a solemn face
and brown eyes as sad and mournful as a spaniel's. The
fourth oarsman was a lithe Creole who moved like a cat, and
even purred like one when he talked. Cap'n Abijah Crabbe
stood on top of the cabin with the handle of the long steering sweep in his hands. From this post of vantage he could
keep one eye on the oarsmen and the other alert for ob-
structions in the water ahead. Navigating the clumsy, forty-
foot craft among the other boats in the narrow creek was
a job that called for a sure hand.

As they moved steadily down the creek and out into the
Ohio, Cap suddenly ducked his head. The eight armed

Limestoners had appeared at the river's edge and were closely scanning the boat. Without seeming to notice them, Abijah touched the steering sweep and swung the boat so the starboard oarsmen were hidden by the cabin.

"They must be lookin' fer somebody," he said.

"Could be," Cap agreed. "There's a lot of scoundrels back in the woods."

"Not near as many as there is on this here river," the Kentuckian said. "And the Spanish is the biggest scoundr'ls of 'em all."

"How do you make that out?"

"I don't make it out. It jest is. The Ohio's crowded with all the settlers as has been comin' sinst the war ended. And what kin they use fer a road? The old Mrs. Sippi, in course. And what is their market? N'Yurlens, in course. And who owns N'Yurlens? The Spanish, in course. And what do the Spanish do? Charge a high duty fer everything goin' through. They make this law, and they make that law, and a boat can't sell its cargo without it's at their prices. Or they keep it waitin' so long that the owner's profits is all eat up."

Cap Gitchie had been hired to help take a boat down the river, not to worry about what happened to its cargo after it got there. But talking with the pessimistic Kentuckian helped pass the time. "Well," he said, "if there's so many settlers along these rivers, whyn't they march down to New Orleans, and tell the Spanish where to head in?"

"Heh, heh," the Kentuckian laughed dryly. "The Spanish is scairt lest we're goin' to try jest that. That's why they let Wilkinson's boats by with light duty."

"Who's Wilkinson?"

"Prob'bly the worst of the scoundr'ls. He went down to N'Yurlens four years ago, in '87, with a ladin' of terbaccy. The Spanish confiscated it, and Wilkinson dared 'em to keep it. Said he was a gen'ral in the American army, and he'd like 'em to keep his boat and cargo on account that would give him an excuse fer gettin' his army and cleanin' up every greasy Spaniard. Anyhow, he scairt 'em and they says, "Well, Wilkinson, we got each other where the hair's short. S'pose we talk turkey? You do what you kin fer us, and we'll do what we kin fer you. You swear allegiance to Spain and go back up the river. Tell everybody who wants to bring a boat down that if they swear allegiance to Spain, they kin get by fer fifteen per cent duty 'stead of twenty-five. Tell anybody as wants to settle on Spanish land that they kin do it. Lemme tell you, them Spanish is scairt. They're scairt we're goin' to come down and kick 'em out."

"And did Wilkinson swear allegiance to Spain?"

"Sure. Most people as goes down the river does."

"What about the United States?"

The Kentuckian shrugged. "That's a long haul away from N'Yurlens. Besides, you don't have to stay Spanish. If'n you take a flatboat down the river, natcher'lly you can't row it back up on account flatboats don't row upcurrent. So you sell or give the boat away after you've sold the cargo, and walk up the Natchez Trace, back into the States. If'n you go down in a keelboat, you row back up. You kin allus unswear after you're out of Spanish country."

Cap Gitchie chuckled. The situation was not too full of either ideals or ethics, but it did have its practical side.

Abijah Crabbe scowled. "It's no laughin' matter, mister. This country has got to have a free and open river, clear to the Gulf!"

"Well, I sure hope you get it," said Cap amiably. He turned to the Kentuckian again. "Are there any fightin' roosters down the river?"

"Sometimes you'd think there wasn't nothin' but," replied the Kentuckian dolefully. "All them Spanish got 'em, and most of the settlers. Kin your rooster fight?"

"Can he fight! He's the red-roarin'est, peel-haul-in'est, scrappin'est, maddest, fastest, fightin'est thing that ever grew feathers! He can lick his weight in hound dogs, wild-cats, and Spaniards."

"We'll have fun," the Kentuckian said, as though that were a very dismal prospect.

The red rooster walked nonchalantly around the deck, peered into the cabin, and experimentally pecked at the Irishman's moccasins. Then he flew up to the cabin roof, cocked a bright eye at Abijah Crabbe, and flew down to cuddle up beside his owner. The feline Creole followed his every move, his eyes reflecting the love of a good fighting cock that had been born in his heart. He turned to smile at Cap Gitchie.

"That ees fine bird," he purred. "I, Baptiste Amante, say so."

The Irishman nodded. "Me old man told me when I left Dublin, 'Mike, never bet on cock fights; they'll ruin ye.' Up to now, he's been right. But I have a feelin' that red bird will bring us luck."

"Bad luck," the Kentuckian said gloomily.

The Irishman laughed, and struck up a song:

The boatman is a lucky man,
No one can do as the boatman can,

The boatmen dance and the boatmen sing,
The boatman is up to everything.

Hi-ho, away we go,
Floating down the O-hi-o.

They anchored that night to some willows below an out-jutting headland. They rowed the boat up to the trees, made it fast, then paid off line until they floated free in the current, far enough out so a sudden fall of water would not leave them stranded. While the Creole cooked a savory gumbo over an open fire in a sand-filled box, the Irishman sang songs of the old country. The night was warm, and they slept on deck, under the stars, while the river gurgled and rolled steadily past them.

They rowed on day after day, passing more cumbersome flatboats and barges on the way, and waving to the settlers who had built their rough-hewn homes on both sides of the river. There was scarcely a day when they did not see some kind of settlement, and often plowed fields gleamed richly black among the stumps of trees. Still the settlers came, having started from as far away as Olean, New York, guiding their craft down the Allegheny to enter the Ohio at Pittsburgh. Men, women, children, horses, cattle, hogs, chickens, and farm implements occupied these floating arks impartially, and all used the river to arrive in this promised land to which they were journeying. But the *River Belle* was a fast boat, bound for New Orleans with a cargo of furs, and could not tarry long for visits.

They were many days out of Louisville, and well below the settlements, gliding between high stone cliffs that bor-

dered both sides of the river, when Abijah Crabbe left his
place at the steering sweep to place an extra horn of powder
and pouch of bullets beside each man.

"What's comin'?" Cap Gitchie asked curiously.

"Cave-in-Rock," the gloomy Kentuckian asserted, as
though that in itself was sufficient explanation.

Abijah climbed back to the top of the cabin, and guided
the *River Belle* out to the center of the river. The mystified
Cap continued to pull on his oar, until from the western
bank floated an agonized appeal.

"Help! For God's sake, help!"

Cap turned his head to see a white man running franti-
cally along the riverbank. His buckskin clothing hung in
ragged shreds from his gaunt frame. A breechcoth was
draped about his thighs, and his beard fluttered as he ran
along the bank, parallel to the keelboat. Again the agonized, heart-wringing cry floated out over the water.

"Help! Help me! Take me on board! I've just escaped
from the Indians."

Without flicking an eyelid or changing his melancholy
expression, the Kentuckian let his oar rest in its lock, picked
up the rifle that lay beside him, took careful aim over the
rail, and squeezed the trigger. The pleading man on the
bank took two more running steps, then two slow ones. His
knees buckled, and he pitched forward, to lie motionless
on the shore. Cap rose in his seat, hot anger inflaming his
face.

"Why, you—"

"Sit down!" came Abijah Crabbe's commanding voice
from over his head.

There was a wild yell from the bank. A long canoe with
twelve Indians in it put out from the cove where it had

been hidden, and bore down on the *River Belle*. Sitting calmly on top of the cabin, for he could not desert the steering sweep, Abijah Crabbe picked up a musket and shot. The foremost Indian dropped his paddle to slump backward against the next man. A rattle of rifle fire came from the canoe, but the bullets thudded against the stout hull of the *River Belle* or splashed in the water nearby. No longer in doubt, Cap knelt beside the rail, sighted on another Indian, and saw him drop. He was aware of other rifles cracking beside him. The canoe hesitated, then put back toward shore. Just at that moment, the red rooster, excited by the noise and confusion, flapped his wings and crowed.

"You!" Abijah Crabbe called imperiously. "You, rooster man! Come on up here!"

Cap rose and climbed the ladder leading to the cabin roof. The little captain's beard worked up and down in indignation. His mild blue eyes glowed. "Is this yer first trip down the river?" he demanded.

"Yup."

"I thought so!" Abijah Crabbe sputtered. "Let me tell ye something, mister—"

"Could you sort of gentle yourself down before you tell it? I never did like being hollered at."

The captain calmed down. "It wa'nt yer fault. Ye didn't know any better. But that white man was a renegade. He wanted to toll us into the bank so's those Indians could climb our hump for us. They try the same thing every time we pass Cave-in-Rock, and other places, too. Don't ever pick up anybody who hollers at ye from this riverbank, and don't stop a man who knows what he's doin' better'n ye do."

"I won't," Cap said mildly. "But it don't do any harm to give a man a little warnin'. What's Cave-in-Rock?"

"It's a big natural cave where river pirates—renegades and Cherokees, mostly—meet and store the plunder they've taken from simple folks who believe all they hear. Ye got to go down river a couple of times before ye get on to all the dodges—like tollin' boats in to the bank. They get lots of 'em, too."

"I reckon so," Cap said, abashed.

He returned to his seat to find the red rooster standing on its edge, clucking to himself. The pantherlike Creole was gazing at him in frank admiration.

"It ees lucky rooster," he said softly. "Nev-aire before have I pass Cave-in-Rock without somebody killed or wounded."

Cap Gitchie swept his oar back, while a happy little grin lighted his face. He seldom had much of an idea where he was going next, or what he was going to do after he got there. But this river life was not a bad one, at all. A man didn't have to wear the seat of his pants out on some office stool, or wonder too much about where his next excitement was coming from.

"What else is on the river?" he asked the Kentuckian.

"Everything," was the gloomy reply. "Pirates, and war parties, and snags, and sand bars, and ignor'nt young fellers that jump up and holler in keelboats. It's a wicked river."

The rooster perched contentedly beside him, and the Kentuckian eyed him thoughtfully. There were such things as good and bad omens. Hadn't he himself, while crossing Kentucky two years before, seen a good omen when the

crescent moon had pointed exactly toward Louisville? He
had gone there, instead of pursuing his plan of heading
down to Eddyville, on the Cumberland. Had he gone to
Eddyville, he would have run square into a big war party,
and no doubt by this time his scalp would be waving before
the lodge of some dusky forest prince.

"I dunno but what I'm glad you've got the bird, son,"
he admitted almost cheerfully.

Cap grinned.

Two nights later they anchored in a quiet little eddy below another point of land. Flatboats and keelboats of every
description—some of the latter going up the river instead
of down—were met there. Cap counted twenty-one craft,
and gazed curiously at the crowd that had gathered on the
shore. The passengers of all the boats were intermingling
freely around the cooking fires; and men, women, and children were dancing to the music a bearded, one-eyed giant,
who looked like a pirate, was coaxing from a violin. A tall
backwoodsman made his way up the bank and stepped on
board the *River Belle*. He eyed the red rooster appraisingly.

"Who owns that thar fowl?" he demanded.

"I do," Cap said proudly.

"I'll bet," the backwoodsman stated, "that he ain't as
good as my dominicker."

"How much you want to bet?"

"A cask of terbaccy, ten beaver pelts, and a ham."

The red rooster was better than the dominicker.

The weather became hot, and the river dropped a little.
The banks that it had flooded bore mute testimony to all
the cargo beside boats that this mighty water carried.
Trees, wrecked boats, buffalo carcasses, great fish, small

fish, drowned deer and elk, and all the other flotsam that a river will carry lay drying on the muddy, cracking banks. Watching it, the Kentuckian's gloom deepened.

"You'll see many a thing cast up there," he said prophetically. "Mebbe, before it's finished, all the men and women who've come to settle above us will be there, too."

"Don't be so happy about things," Cap Gitchie admonished. "You're such an optimist, Kentucky, that a man would think nothing bad ever happened to you."

The Irishman guffawed and the Creole chuckled, while up on the cabin roof, even Abijah Crabbe smiled to himself as he stood with the steering sweep in his hands and studied the river ahead. He had been down it many times, but it was never the same river twice in succession. There were always new islands born where none had been before, and islands swept away that had stood for years. It was a changeable river, a restless and ever-searching one that was continually trying new patterns and new directions. It was as changeable as life itself, thought Abijah. And while he stood on top of the cabin, steering the *River Belle,* he reflected on the course of his own life.

Back in Philadelphia, so many years ago that it now seemed as though it never could have been, he had been a schoolteacher. Before the war, his world had been a safe, well-ordered place wherein he had made the sons and daughters of the well-to-do ready to further their education in England or France. Every morning he had started out from his own modest little home, and every night he had returned to find his wife and three children awaiting him there. But that had been before the plague. . . .

Then had come the war for independence, but he had seen little of it. With his family gone, he had had to go. He could not stay in a place that reminded him of what had been. The frontier, a whole world away from Philadelphia, was where he had found forgetfulness. And there seemed to be nothing taken away without at least partial compensation. In the years he had been traveling up and down the western rivers, he had seen a continent come to life.

First there had been silent, buckskinned men, who would never even venture out the door without their long rifles. Then had come wild and roaring men, sober and industrious men, shiftless men, men with initiative, men stained with every crime in the calendar. But regardless of their other characteristics, the men who had opened this raw western country had had one thing in common—the courage to try something new. And they were not only trying it, but were doing it. They raised their crops, and gathered their fruits, and trapped their furs, and sent them down the broad rivers, down to New Orleans. Down there the Spanish sat across their outlet to the sea, but if they tried to impose too many restrictions. . . . The river would have to be open and free to all men. And it would be, sooner or later. He had even heard that there were already negotiations between Gayoso, the Spanish Governor, and the infant government of the United States.

Abijah Crabbe looked down at his crew, his lined face softening. If the men who came here were courageous and daring, they were also simple. That youngster with the gamecock, who had been in such a hurry to get away from Louisville, the glum Kentuckian, the easygoing Creole, the gay Irishman . . . their fetish was a red rooster, their aim to see what happened when and if they reached New Orleans. The day was the thing, and so long as the sun rose, all was well.

Yes, they were a simple breed of people, these folks who had gathered from every corner of the earth to make a highway of this broad river. The wilderness had never seen their like, and probably never would again. Simple they were, but they still had their smouldering passions that a careless word or gesture could fan into leaping fire. Then God help whomever or whatever got in their way. They stood by themselves, and never dreamed of asking anyone else to help them. And if they wanted something, they would never count the cost of getting it.

A smile twitched the corners of his lips as he listened to their heated discussion of the rooster's good and bad points. No doubt the bird would fight again at New Madrid, and at Chickasaw Bluffs, and at Walnut Hills, and at Natchez, and at whatever settlers' cabins were near where they tied up. If he won all these fights, he would become a mighty creature, part of the river tradition, and boatmen would boast about his prowess as long as any of them might live.

The rooster did fight, and win, until Abijah Crabbe steered his craft into the bustling port of Natchez. He saw the Governor's ornate barge anchored beside a heavily armed gunboat and two supply ships. A small boat with Spanish soldiers in it put out from the barge and came toward the *River Belle*. Five uniformed dragoons and a dapper young officer boarded the keelboat to look over her papers and cargo.

With only a cursory glance at the Spanish ships, Cap Gitchie had repaired to the *River Belle's* cabin to sleep as soon as they tied up at Natchez. The cabin was musty with the odor of baled furs, and the aroma of the previous cargoes it had held still mingled faintly with this newer, stronger one. Cap stretched out in a cleared space, and drowsily listened to the Spanish soldiers board the boat. For a moment he hovered halfway between sleep and wakefulness, wondering if it would be worth his while to go out for another look. But the soldiers would be there in the morning, and the *River Belle* was going to New Orleans anyhow. There he would see more than enough of Spanish soldiers. He dropped off into dreamless and untroubled sleep.

When he awoke it was dark, and he went on deck to see the lamps of Natchez shining palely in the distance. To-night he would go into town with his red rooster and let him fight the best the Spanish, or the French, or whoever was in control, had to offer. His eyes sought the stern of the *River Belle,* where the Kentuckian, the Creole, the Irish-man, and Abijah Crabbe were gathered about the cooking pot that hung over the sand-heaped firebox. Cap walked toward them.

"What's the matter?" he asked. "Ain't there any inns in this Natchez, where we can get a civilized meal for once?"

"Ho, ho," the Creole said softly. "You are indeed *l'enfant,* my friend."

"He jest don't know about Natchez," the glum Ken-tuckian amended. "Sure, we could find a place to eat. And they'd bring us a stinkin' mess of slumgullion a dog wouldn't eat. Then they'd say, 'Twenty reales, See-nyors,'— that's what they call folks down in this neck o' the woods —and when we wouldn't pay it they'd call their sojers to have us thrown in jail."

"Well. . . ." Cap looked wistfully toward the shore. "There's five of us, ain't there?"

"I've got a cargo of fur to look out for," Abijah Crabbe said sharply. "I can't risk it."

"All right, cap'n. But I'm goin' to take the rooster over there tonight and see what we can stir up."

The Creole's white teeth flashed in the darkness, and the Irishman chuckled with anticipation. Cap walked over to his shipped oar, upon the handle of which the rooster had been in the habit of spending the night, and reached down in the darkness so the bird could step onto his hand. Nothing moved. The customary little rustle of feathers was missing. Surprised, Cap straightened up, then tried the handles of the other oars, one by one. He walked back to the cooking fire.

"What happened to the rooster?" he demanded.

The Kentuckian, noisily chewing a succulent bit of meat, stopped eating, his mouth half open. The four boatmen looked at each other, the ruddy glow cast by the fire outlining in sharp relief the hard intent features.

The Irishman spoke up. "I ain't seen the bird since the Spaniards left. I thought he was with you."

Cap Gitchie stood still in the darkness, while anger crawled the length of his spine. He looked at the Governor's barge, riding softly at anchor while wavelets lapped her heavy hull. Without a word he entered the cabin to pick up his tomahawk, and when he came out the Kentuckian, the Creole, and the Irishman gathered about him. Abijah Crabbe looked steadily over the rail. He turned once, but did not speak when the four men drew the *River Belle* in to the bank and stepped ashore. Nothing that he could say or do would hold them now. Their luck had gone.

For a moment they stood on the dark shore, looking

vengefully toward the Governor's barge, then started down the riverbank to where half a dozen pirogues were drawn up. Slowly, so as to make no noise, they launched one and climbed in. The Creole, handling the stern paddle, dipped it as softly as a cat flicking out a sheathed claw to catch a mouse.

The dark mass of the Governor's barge loomed above them, and a sharp, Spanish voice broke the silence. *"Hola?"*

The Creole worked the pirogue up to the bow of the barge, keeping in the shadow of the hull. Cap silently climbed up the anchor chain and peeped over the deck. Just before him, scarcely a yard away, a uniformed sentry stood with one hand on his cutlass, peering toward the dark stern. The night was hot, and he had taken off his helmet. Cap swung the flat of his tomahawk, and with a soft little thud the sentry melted down to mingle with the shadows on the deck.

From the other end of the barge a questioning voice demanded, "Juan! What is happening?"

Running softly on moccasined feet, the four intruders entered the dimly lighted cabin and swung the door shut behind them. The Creole dropped the heavy latch into place, and stood with his ear to the door, an excited grin on his dark face. The Kentuckian wrapped his long arms about another soldier, who suddenly appeared before them, then released his captive quickly, and swung a fist to his jaw. The Spaniard bounced back, then his sword licked forth and blood stained the Kentuckian's shirt. The Irishman swung the flat of his tomahawk, and the soldier dropped heavily. They raced through the cabin into a larger one with a closed door at the far end. Before they could reach it, five soldiers rose from their card game, reaching wildly for weapons. Cap jumped on the nearest man. . . .

Inside that closed door, Governor Gayoso had for the past hour been in conference with four of his staff officers, and was just finishing a speech.

"The interests of Spain must at all times be nearest my heart. But how shall those interests best be served? Señor Pinckney, of the United States Government, has lately sent a courier to me, saying that he upholds the claim of the American settlers on the upper river for an open, duty-free port in New Orleans. He insists that the traders who bring goods down must have whatever rights of transshipment they desire. Acceding to his wishes would deprive Spain of much revenue, and I do not think this infant American government is prepared to use force. I do not greatly fear the United States, or anything they may do. The real problem is, if we continue to operate this port as a source of royal revenue, and charge such duties as we see fit, will those half-civilized frontiersmen on the upper river take matters into their own hands?"

"They would not dare," a bulky, scar-faced Colonel of Guards said contemptuously. "But suppose they do? We'll drive them back soon enough."

"My good Colonel Perez," Gayoso said, "have you ever fought Kentuckians?"

The Colonel's face flushed. "No. But it would be a pleasure to—"

At that moment the thudding of the gun butts of those soldiers who were trying to break down the outer door rumbled through the room. An excited voice shouted in Spanish, "Open up! I command you." A second later four blood-streaked Americans with tomahawks in their hands burst through the door of the conference room. As one man, the assembled officers rose and drew their swords.

"Keep your shirts on, Governor," said the tallest of the Americans, "and tell your pals to do likewise. There ain't any sense in gettin' yourselves massacreed."

"This is an outrage!" Gayoso sputtered.

"So's stealin' roosters!" Cap Gitchie snarled. "Do I get him back? Or do we bust up your meat house?"

"Do you get what back?"

"My red rooster. The one one of your tinhorn soldiers swiped off the *River Belle* this afternoon."

"Do I understand that one of the Spanish soldiers who boarded your boat today stole from you?"

"Yup. Make up your mind, Governor. We ain't got all night."

"Lieutenant Montez," Gayoso directed, "investigate the boarding parties who were out this afternoon. Find the soldier who stole this man's property. Have it returned, and see that the soldier is punished."

Governor Gayoso sat for a long while after the boatman had gone. It had taken him some little time to reassure himself that this was not the long-feared attack by the backwoodsmen. For it had seemed scarcely credible that four madmen, alone, would dare board the state barge of the Governor of Louisiana. But four men had done it, and if any army composed of similar men ever came. . . .

In his mind he began to construct phrases for an official report, to be sent to His Majesty Charles IV: "In the light of recent firsthand observations . . . it is my considered opinion . . . for the promotion of friendly relations . . . recommendations for free trade along the lower Mississippi, and the opening of the port of New Orleans. . . ."

Cap Gitchie's rooster had won another fight.

STAGE TO YUMA

MARVIN DeVRIES

The reek of trouble reached Tate Ibsen as soon as the stage-coach entered the gorge. He couldn't give it a reason. His searching eyes swept the high rim and the broken walls, and touched nothing but glare and tumbled rock, but he had the feeling there was more up there than he could find. Until he could point it out, however, he wouldn't mention it, but words were on his lips, so he said a few about the heat, something they were all already miserably aware of.

"Just like I imagine hell is going to be. Don't you think so, Miss Quimby?"

Miss Quimby must have heard a lot of blunt talk during the past few days, but it still shocked her. "I—I really don't know," she said, struggling to be civil and critical at the same time.

This was the route to Yuma. Tate Ibsen was one of six passengers. Ordinarily, he would have taken a horse. He didn't like stagecoach travel. Usually, there were soppy children or ladies with the vapors to contend with. But this time he had business aboard and had to face the discomforts.

There were no soppy children, but there was little Miss Quimby, with her faded parasol and reticule, surely good for one vapor, and there was Doc, sagging at the seams and bleary-eyed with booze. Doc, nipping from a fancy bottle, sat next to Ibsen. Miss Quimby, taking no more room than a stick, was in the far corner. Watts, a deputy marshal, and Deuce, his prisoner, who had a stiff leg, sat straight across from Ibsen. The sixth passenger, a Mexican boy dressed up in his best bib and tucker, sat upstairs with the driver. Occasional bursts of barnyard Spanish drifted down from them into the coach. The boy was on his way to a mission school in Faraway, which was Miss Quimby's destination. Ibsen put two and two together, and added it up as one pupil and one teacher.

Waves of furnace heat poured up and invaded the coach. Miss Quimby wiped her gritty cheeks and red eyes with a wadded handkerchief. Doc took another nip. Ibsen could see him considering passing the bottle, but finally deciding against such reckless generosity. The deputy took off his hat and wiped the sweatband with his elbow. The handcuffed prisoner moved his stiff leg and bumped it against Ibsen's boots.

"Sorry," Ibsen said.

Deuce glared and started to say something. The deputy gave him a hard poke and told him to shut up. "Don't bother the passengers."

"I don't," Deuce answered. "They bother me. That big fathead—"

"It's my fault," Ibsen said mildly.

"The hell with it," Deuce flared. "Kick the leg off for all of me. I don't care, leg or no leg. Go ahead."

"No, thanks," Ibsen said. "You might need it more than you think."

"Yeah, on a rock pile."

Miss Quimby bent forward so she could get a good look at the prisoner. "What did you do, my boy?" she asked in a sympathetic voice.

Deuce leaned across toward her and whispered, "Murder." He raised his handcuffed hands and drew a finger across his throat. "You know—zzt!—with a knife. But I didn't do it."

"At any rate," Ibsen said, "you have a sound reason for coming this way. You can't help yourself. The rest of us, I reckon, just don't have good sense. Doc, what brings you this way, if I may ask?"

Doc twirled his heavy gold chain around his finger and gave the question consideration. A small flush showed on his face. "I'm looking around for a place to locate," he said finally. "A little tired of the usual, you know. How about yourself?" The question was a boomerang his pride had taught him to throw.

"I'll be as honest as you, Doc," Ibsen said. "I have a

friend in Yuma pen and I'm going to try to bust him out."
He turned his sardonic eyes on the deputy for an answer.

"Nobody gets nobody outta Yuma pen," Watts told him.

"Still," Ibsen said mildly, "some try, for friendship's
sake."

Deuce wanted to smoke, and Watts, with elaborate consideration, rolled him one, but when it was finished he
kept it for himself and blew smoke in Deuce's face, grin-
ning at his audience. "I always say nothin's too good for a
man who's bound for Yuma pen. My heart bleeds."

"You have quite a sense of humor," Doc told him. His
voice sounded as though he honestly admired the deputy,
but his eyes rebuked him.

A speech of some kind budded on Ibsen's lips, but he
kept it back, and turned his curiosity on Miss Quimby. "I
understand you're a schoolteacher."

Miss Quimby nodded. The feather on her bonnet dipped
and threw off a spray of dust. "I'm going to teach in Faraway."

"So I heard." Ibsen knew the place. It was a small ragged
settlement, and he believed there weren't more than a half-
dozen children in the whole district. The poor woman
probably had no idea, and he wanted to prepare her a little.
"Even in a little place like that," he told her, "you'll probably find someone who will take to learning. They're anywhere; don't you think so, Doc?"

"Surely," Doc said.

"It's in the nature of missionary work," Miss Quimby
said. "I understand it's very sparsely settled."

She made it sound very satisfactory to her, but Ibsen
looked behind the pride, the same pride that touched Doc,
and could imagine the hidden consternation and dismay

that must engulf her, if not now, at least later when she
got a look at Faraway. He could imagine her more un-
wanted where she came from than wanted at the place
where she was going. It was a retreat of the vanquished, a
last desperate move made with as much pride as she could
hold around her, but it was something she couldn't help any
more than Deuce in his handcuffs could help his trip to
Yuma.

"I'm sure they need you," Ibsen said, putting on a show
of conviction.

" 'Better build schoolrooms for the boy than cells and
gibbets for the man,' " Doc quoted. "Eh, Deuce?"

"Could be," Deuce agreed.

" 'There is only one good,' " Doc quoted again, " 'namely,
knowledge; and only one evil, namely, ignorance.' "

"Diogenes," Miss Quimby said with sudden sparkle.

Doc laughed. "The man with the lantern, and Eliza Cook.
Ma'am, if you can find one youngster anywhere to teach
something to, you are here on a better errand than any of
us. Don't you agree, Ibsen?"

Buttering her up, too, Ibsen thought, but he nodded
agreement. "At any rate, ma'am, we'll see that you get
there, won't we, Doc?"

Doc grinned. "She and the boy up there, the hope of the
future."

The next time Tate Ibsen scanned the walls he saw what
he was looking for, the glint of sun on a brown arm dan-
gling over a rock. It drew back while he looked, like a snake
into its den, and he couldn't find it again, but it was time
to speak up. He let some time go past, as little and as much
as he dared, then called up to the driver to stop. There was

always an obvious reason for such occasions, and Boggs came to a stop.

He got down himself, giving the reins to the proud Mexican boy. Ibsen walked away, motioning him to follow. When they were out of earshot, he told the driver what he had seen.

Boggs wasn't impressed. "They never bother me," he said. "Besides, there ain't none hereabouts."

"I saw one," Ibsen insisted.

Boggs exploded, "One Apache, good or bad, don't make an ambush."

"At any rate," Ibsen said, "I think the boy ought to get inside, and I'll get up there with you, at least till we get through the gorge."

The boy surrendered his place reluctantly, and Boggs promised him he could come back out later. "This gent needs a little air, is all."

He climbed up, and Ibsen took the other side. The gorge was roughly funnel-shaped. They were close to the narrowest section. The road was nearest the south wall. Ibsen, scanning the heights, saw another brown figure, and reached for his gun. Before he could use it, the whisper of an arrow went past his ear. It struck the driver and dug deep between his ribs near the armpit. He lurched off the seat before Ibsen could grab him, and toppled headfirst to the ground. Another arrow struck a lead mule and dropped it. The rest piled up in a snarl of harness. No more arrows were shot, no more brown men appeared.

Ibsen grabbed the shotgun that was up there and jumped down. He took Boggs' hand gun and put both weapons inside the coach. "Don't anyone get out," he warned. "Keep away from the openings. If they come down, let 'em have it as fast as you know how."

In spite of his order, Doc stepped out and took a look at Boggs. "I'm no good with a gun, but this is my line."

"I'm afraid not. It's past you." Ibsen moved forward, trying to quiet the mules.

The shot animal was dead. Ibsen cut the traces and hooked up the other lead mule, harness to harness with the dead brute, and got the road cleared. Then another arrow whistled down, and another mule dropped. The rest panicked. The two wheelers wound up facing the coach, one on its knees, the other with its legs over the whiffletree. Ibsen used his knife, cutting leather where it had to be cut, then got back into the coach.

The boy shoved over to the middle and sat between Doc and Ibsen. Watts' hands were shaking. Ibsen studied him awhile and wrote him off as a dead loss. "Two of the mules are dead," he announced. "The rest are all snarled up, and the harness is torn to shreds. If we get out of here at all, it will have to be on foot, but for the time being we'll sit tight. It's good cover against arrows, and it seems as if that's all they have up there."

Miss Quimby opened her reticule and got out some smelling salts and held them to her nose. After one deep sniff, she offered them around.

"Later maybe, ma'am," Ibsen said, and dared anyone to laugh. He studied the walls of the gorge and told the boy to look, thinking his young eyes might be sharper, but neither of them could see any life.

"Watts, won't you have a nip of this?" Doc asked, carefully hiding the reason for his offer.

Watts drank it, gratefully and long.

"Ye gods," Doc breathed, "don't run me clear out."

The boy put his hands flat together between his legs as if he meant to sit it out that way. He was quiet and very attentive to everything that went on, but he didn't seem to be afraid. Miss Quimby, too, had made up her mind to be brave. This was death, and she meant to face it like a lady, smelling salts handy.

Ibsen pushed his hat back and scratched his head. "They'd come down if they were strong enough to risk it. There must be just a few of them on a spree. What they've done so far looks like plain teasing. Otherwise, they'd have shot me instead of that mule. They're having an afternoon's fun."

"We got to get outta here," Watts mumbled, gasping for breath.

Deuce laughed in his face, and got another poke.

"You'll have to turn him loose, Watts," Ibsen said. "We may need him." He got out Boggs' big gun and tried to hand it to Deuce.

Watts struck it down. "Keep that gun away from him. What you think you're doing?"

"I'm trying to take a good look at what we're up against here," Ibsen said, without losing patience. "I don't like to get bossy, but I can, and I will if I must."

"Not with me."

"What do you think, Doc?"

Doc pursed his lips. "I want to ask a question. I have the impression that you're aboard here to help Deuce escape. That fuss about leg room didn't ring true to me somehow. It seems to me we ought to know what takes precedence here—our lives, or helping Deuce escape, if that's what you're at."

Ibsen hesitated with an answer, but he finally nodded. "That's what I'm here for. I have horses staked out at the end of the gorge, ready for a getaway. Deuce is a friend of mine. He's also the best shot I ever saw. That's why I want him turned loose. Right now, that's all that counts."

Watts didn't wait for Doc's opinion. He raised his gun and told Ibsen to go.

Ibsen didn't move. "No, I won't get out," he stated, "but I'll guarantee this much. You turn Deuce loose, and when this is over you can handcuff him again and we'll start from scratch."

Watts wouldn't listen. "Get out. Head that way." He canted his head to the far wall. "There's nobody on that side."

Doc settled it with the bottle. As inconspicuously as possible he got a good grip on the neck and gave Watts a hard whack across the arm. The gun dropped, and Ibsen recovered it. "O.K., that's fine, Doc," he said.

"I'm good with a bottle," Doc admitted modestly. "To tell you the truth, I want to keep you around a while. I shouldn't have asked the question. It was idle."

Ibsen unlocked the handcuffs. He gave Deuce the big gun and let Watts have his own back. He wanted Doc to take the shotgun, but Doc shook his head and said the boy could do better.

"What's your name, anyway, son?"

The boy said it was Porfio, after a dead uncle.

"Can you handle a shotgun?"

"*Si.*"

"All right. If they come down on us, blast away. But

wait until they're close. That's the only way that weapon's any good."

"I know," Porfio said.

"Sorry about the fuss," Ibsen told Miss Quimby.

She gave him a speechless nod.

"Incidentally, there's nothing the matter with Deuce's leg," Ibsen went on. "He was shot, but it's all healed up. He was hanging onto it so Watts would think he couldn't move fast."

An arrow snapped against the coach to remind them of their troubles. Ibsen scanned the rim and the pockets of gloom in the walls. The mules moved farther away, their hoofs clattering. A wild taunting screech came down and Miss Quimby shuddered visibly and propped her wadded handkerchief against her mouth. Still another arrow came down, breaking through the roof.

Ibsen's conviction that the ambush was a flimsy one continued to grow. Still, there was a strong possibility the raiders would quit their fooling and close in for loot. They surely would after dark, he felt. He put no faith in the dubious saw that Apaches would not attack by night. "Those horses I mentioned are in a little box meadow at the end of the gorge," he explained. "There's a rope across the mouth. Porfio, can you catch a horse with a rope?"

"Si, señor."

"How about you, Doc?"

"No. None of this is my dish, Ibsen, but don't bother about it. Concentrate on Miss Quimby and the boy. That school, you know."

Porfio lifted his eyes. "I would not like for anyone to worry himself about me because of how old I am," he announced gravely.

Doc grinned. "You see what I mean, Ibsen?" He turned to Miss Quimby. "Take that one by the hand, ma'am, and go your way."

Miss Quimby's eyes melted. The thin face took on a glow. "Doctor," she said, leaving all her fears behind for a moment, "sometimes I think they have more to keep than to learn, but I teach what I can."

This was spoken from the heart, with deep humility, and her squeaky voice didn't spoil the words. Somewhere, deep down inside of her, was a dedicated purpose and the stanch bright hope that something must come of it as surely as day came out of night.

"Ma'am," Doc said, "I wish I could be young again." He overlaid the words with his usual dry look, so it was hard to tell whether he meant them or not.

To Ibsen, this was more Diogenes-Eliza Cook talk, but he saw the point. Most men spoiled their lives before they used up their span; Watts with his fears, Doc with his booze, Deuce with his temper, himself with his disdain, all with something they had found along the way. Especially, he thought, Watts with his sorry fears.

He shifted his position and searched the north wall again. "Nothing going on over there," he remarked. "I wonder. If there's nothing up there, we'd be in pretty good shape, once we got under that overhang."

"If we could get out of range from this side," Doc commented.

"I think that's possible, but it wouldn't do much good if we ran head-on into more on the other side."

Watts leaned forward and took a look. He searched the far wall carefully from top to bottom and side to side. Ibsen stared at him with mild disdain, knowing what he had put into his head. Deuce gave Ibsen a puzzled look. Ibsen shook his head briefly, warning Deuce to mind his own business. Deuce looked at Doc, and both their eyes went blank.

"No use everybody risking their necks," Watts stated finally, all his rancor gone. "I'll give it a try."

"I wouldn't ask you to," Ibsen said.

"That's not the point," Watts insisted. "Somebody's got to find out if it's clear over there."

It sounded generous, especially after the rumpus they had had, but the deputy couldn't quite hide the cunning look in his eyes, the avid look of a coward grabbing for his life at the expense of the others.

"Of course," Ibsen said, "there's always the chance there's some up there."

"Of course," Watts agreed, much too quickly to give the warning any thought. He obviously didn't believe it. "I'll take the risk."

Ibsen nodded. "All right then. We'll watch this wall and try to stop them from opening up on you from behind."

The deputy climbed down in the silence. He hesitated for some time in the protection of the coach, then started to run, zigzagging like a giddy snipe until he was out of range, when he slowed down.

"I hope you know he's running out on us," Deuce muttered.

"He's trying to, that's sure."

Watts didn't make the crossing. Ibsen saw the arrow come down and strike him in the chest. The deputy went down over a block of black lava and didn't move again.

"You knew it all the time, didn't you?" Deuce remarked.

Ibsen shook his head. "I didn't know."

"Any fool could guess."

"Guessing wasn't good enough. We know now, and we're stuck with it."

"Do you actually have horses out there?" Doc inquired. "Or was that just bait for Watts?"

"The horses are there."

Doc sagged back in his seat and stared regretfully at the spilled whisky. "But it was still bait. I don't think I could do that, Ibsen. I'm not critical. I only mean to say I would rather go myself than send another."

"I didn't do it in fun, Doc. I'm trying to figure out a way to get at least some of us out of here alive."

"Miss Quimby and the boy?"

"Maybe. You say they're the top items. In a pinch, Watts would have run out on them."

"I agree we could probably spare him better than anyone, including myself. We all saw what he was, I think, but still a man can be a coward under one circumstance and a brave man under another."

"We have only one circumstance here," Ibsen stated roughly.

"Why didn't you send me?"

"That may come, Doc."

The words had a tired, regretful sound, but they had to be spoken, because they were the bitter fruit of hard, relentless thought. A man in mortal danger stripped himself down to bare essentials. He used what came to hand to save what he could, and let the rest go. He scouted for possible loopholes of escape, and if they were closed he turned to something else. Pick and choose.

But even without Doc's Diogenes-Eliza Cook talk, Ibsen held the deepest conviction that he was charged with saving Miss Quimby and the boy beyond all others. The reasons were vague. A man could say the weak and helpless were wards of the strong, but anyone put to the test could quibble with such a statement. However, he couldn't quibble with his conviction, and now that he had learned the way out was blocked, he cast about for another possible move.

"I think the thing that bothers them up there," he thought aloud, "is that they don't know how many of us there are down here. To me that means there are fewer of them than could reasonably get into a coach like this."

"They want odds, and they don't know what they got," Deuce said.

Ibsen nodded. "There might be six—eight—ten up there."

"We could handle that many if they only came down and made a fight," Deuce claimed.

"Speaking of odds," Ibsen went on, "so far as they know, there's just one man and a boy in here. They saw the driver and the boy, and you and me, Doc."

"And Watts," Doc put in.

"Yes, but I'm assuming they wouldn't notice the difference between me and Watts, so they saw four, and two are dead. A man and a boy left. That ought to put the odds in their favor enough to tempt them down. We'll wait and see."

"S'pose it doesn't?" Doc said.

"Then we ought to give them bigger odds."

They waited a long time. Doc picked up the empty bottle, took a long caressing look through the amber glass, then dropped it over the edge. It made a little explosion when it hit. Sweat stung Deuce's raw wrists, and he blew on them to keep them cool. Miss Quimby used her smelling salts again, and the sharp fumes engulfed them all. An arrow snapped against the coach.

"Hurry, hurry, hurry, the man says," Doc commented.

"We're in a bigger hurry than they are," Ibsen stated, "but as soon as it gets dark they'll come down and pour it on. That makes it bad. They have bows and arrows, and you can't fight bows and arrows in the dark. They give you nothing to shoot at."

"If it's odds they want, I'll dig out," Deuce volunteered. "I could make a better job of it than Watts."

"No," Ibsen told him. "You're the best shot here. You stay to the last."

"You're aiming at me," Doc said.

"I guess I am, Doc."

"All right. Let's hear it."

"I'd like to make it look as if you and the boy are the last ones left in here. The two of you could get into an argument about pulling out. You want to go, and he's afraid to make the try. You get out and haul him with you. Make it a big argument. They'll be curious and apt to hold their fire till it's over. It's a risk for the boy, but if you make it a big show, I think it will work. If I were up there watching, I believe I would come to the conclusion that you were the only man left. In the end, Porfio pulls free and gets back in here. You go on and make out the best you can."

"It all sounds very logical," Doc finally spoke up without a quaver. "Surely, the boy ought to be the last to go. He was the last to come." His smile ranged toward Miss Quimby. "And he ought to have someone to take him by the hand. You see, ma'am, most of us have had our little say. If there was any good in it, you tell the boy. That's how things go on. It all makes good sense."

Miss Quimby swallowed several times, like a dry pump, before she could get out a word. "I—I don't know." Dismay engulfed her, as if here at last she had to look at what she was and what she ought to be. "I don't know," she breathed again. "What can one say that means enough?"

"By the time this is over, ma'am," Doc said gently, "I should think you will know all there is to say."

"I better go," Deuce begged, looking at Ibsen.

Ibsen shook his head.

"I'm curious," Doc said. "S'pose you had to give odds right down the line?"

"I've told you Deuce is the best shot. It's no game, Doc."

"H'm," Doc said. "Well, son." With a few grunts and groans, as though age were the worst of his troubles, he worked up steam and stepped outside, pulling Porfio along.

Ibsen wouldn't look. Miss Quimby clutched her embroidered reticule and the knob of her parasol until her knuckles turned white. Deuce watched the wall. Doc and Porfio bickered awhile, but Porfio finally broke away and climbed back into the safety of the coach. Doc, with an exasperated gesture that indicated he had done all he could, walked away alone.

Deuce spat out an oath and raised his gun. Ibsen batted it down. "Stay back out of sight," he ordered. "You know what the idea is."

"I see one. He's gettin' set to—"

Doc grunted suddenly. Ibsen heard him go down. Miss Quimby gasped and put her hands over her eyes.

"I could've stopped that," Deuce flared. "You—"

"No more talk," Ibsen ordered. "If there's anything to say, whisper it. Don't show yourself either."

Doc started moving again. Ibsen heard his boots dragging. He was probably traveling on all fours. Another swift whoosh and thump brought him to a halt. He called out something that got lost in his throat. Miss Quimby tried to get out, but Ibsen pushed her back. Doc wasn't heard from again.

Ibsen had a great capacity for calmness, and it stood him in good stead now. It was wait, wait, wait, and nothing else, while the sun moved away, and the shapes and shadows in the gorge changed. Deuce was boiling, and Miss Quimby nursed sharp resentments and antagonisms. A wild whoop bickered through the gorge, and Ibsen saw a stirring along the south wall. Deuce saw it too and whispered an oath.

Ibsen picked them out one by one, counting eight; three from the north wall and five from the south. For good measure, he added one from behind and one from ahead, but those he couldn't see. He assumed they would be there to make a tight ambush. He told Miss Quimby to get down to the floor between the seats, and he put Porfio on his knees behind her. "Lay the gun over her back," he instructed. "That'll steady it. Don't shoot till I say so. You've got to get two the first shot. Deuce, you keep your temper. It's got to be a big slaughter all at once."

Deuce flattened out on the seat, facing the north wall. Ibsen, on the other seat, faced the other way. With as much consideration as he could muster, Porfio placed the gun along the slant of Miss Quimby's back, the tip resting on the edge of the door.

The Apaches made no further attempt at concealment. They laughed and crowed as they came, but they halted before getting into range, and Ibsen thought he had failed in spite of all his precautions.

"On top," Deuce breathed. "There's one on top."

Ibsen looked up and saw the roof splinter. A stone blade showed through, then a steely eye. Ibsen fired straight up. A hair-raising shriek came back at him, then a clatter and thump, and the Apache slid over the edge and toppled to the ground.

The rest charged, and arrows hissed in through the openings. "Let 'em come, let 'em come," Ibsen told himself until they were all in point-blank range. Then he poked Porfio, and the scatter-gun roared. Deuce's gun joined in, and his own, and smoke simmered out through the openings, and arrows swept in.

One raider reached the door, and Ibsen shot him in the face before he could use his club or get the door open. Wails of anger and surprise and agony went up. The fight all went Ibsen's way, except that Deuce didn't keep his temper. Something happened on his side that brought it to a boil, and he lunged out the door before Ibsen could stop him. He couldn't look either. He was too busy on his own side.

The attack came and went like a roll of thunder in the sky. All at once, there were no more Apaches to shoot at. The wild fury died. Ibsen took a wary look and called Deuce, but he didn't get an answer. He got out and saw Deuce lying on the ground near Boggs and a dead Apache. Evidently, the Apache had tried to scalp Boggs. The sight had set Deuce on fire, and it had cost him his life.

Ibsen bent down and picked up the big gun that had belonged to Boggs and put it in his pants' belt. "Doc'll think I welshed sure," Ibsen's lips moved around the words, but no sound came. "Tell him the facts, Deuce, if you two get together. I'd like to have him know."

He walked around and counted heads, and called Miss

Quimby and Porfio. "No time to lose," he told them. "I made a count, and I think two got away. Let's travel, before they block us again."

The meadow where Ibsen had left his horses was a small enclosed place with a scattering of dry grass and a water seep. The walls were high, coming down to the floor in a series of rock terraces. He had stretched a rope across the mouth. The saddles were hidden nearby.

The horses came readily to hand, and Ibsen wasted no time getting Miss Quimby and the boy aboard, and on their way to the gate. He was desperately pinched for time. The two Apaches who had escaped were trailing them, and their obvious intention was to block the narrow opening to the meadow. Ibsen had no more deputies or doctors to dole out, only himself, if he meant to go that far.

It was far to go for anyone who had no desire to travel a glory road. But he did owe Doc a forfeit, unless, of course, he wanted to say that Doc, with his fast talk, was at the bottom of it all. It could be said. Doc had seen Ibsen go to work on Watts, baiting him out of the coach with smooth talk, and Doc had taken hold of it and made it something of his own, throwing out bait that Ibsen thought was his own fine say until at last Doc had his word to save the saints and let the sinners go. That much could be said without throwing reason to the winds, and it left Ibsen with a choice. A man had the right to draw back from cunning and trickery, and make his own way from where he stood when he discovered it. But it was getting late, too late. He stopped the horses short of the gate and pointed up. "There they are."

"*Si, señor,*" Porfio said, his voice as quiet and steady as ever. "I see them."

"I'll climb up and try to get at them from behind. I'll yell when it's safe to move. When you hear me, clear out. Don't wait for me. Miss Quimby, can you hang onto that horse?"

"I shall try," Miss Quimby said.

Ibsen considered giving Porfio one of the guns, but decided against it. Boggs' big-calibered weapon had only one cartridge left, and Ibsen couldn't spare the other one where he was going. With a last word to wait for his signal, he walked away.

At first, the climb was easy. He made a wide circle to keep out of range, but he made no effort at concealment. Most of the time it took care of itself. Miss Quimby and Porfio were in plain view all the time, waiting patiently for his signal, waiting in their deep humility to inherit the earth.

His difficulties increased. Sheer walls faced him, and it was all he could do to claw his way up from terrace to terrace. Boggs' big peacemaker, stuck in his belt, was a nuisance. He holstered his own weapon so he could use both hands. He couldn't see the Apaches, but he had a fix on where they were, and when he thought he was high enough he moved their way. Before he got very far, however, the ledge he was on tapered to nothing, and he had to climb again, up a ten-foot wall.

Here, he lost his gun. Bad footing and hurry did it. Halfway to the top, a rock let go and threw him. He was lucky enough to catch himself on the narrow ledge, but his gun slid out of the holster and went on. Somewhere on its way the hammer hit rock, and the cartridge exploded.

The sound boomed and barked along the terraced walls and gave Miss Quimby's horse a fit. Porfio did what he could, but the animal got away and headed into the gap.

Miss Quimby started to slide off. Porfio cut around in front and caught her mount by the head and brought it to a stop. Miss Quimby slid the rest of the way and hit the ground. An arrow swished down at her, but it fell short.

A little more pull and they'd make it, Ibsen thought. He climbed again. This time he made it and ran along the higher terrace, which brought him into the open two rows above the crouching Apaches.

They didn't hear him. One of them was watching the place where his gun had exploded, the other was stringing another arrow. Down below, Porfio held Miss Quimby's horse and tried to give her a boost into the saddle at the same time, but she was all skirts and couldn't throw her leg across. She couldn't even claw her way up. She made a ridiculous figure to a man who considered the back of a horse the only proper place for anyone to be, a flailing, inept scarecrow too exasperating to take seriously, regardless of Doc's pretty words.

This, then, was the place for a man with only one load in his weapon to stop and think, or, better still, to move on out of reach, and content himself with what he had tried to do. It was still a possibility. The Apaches didn't know he stood behind them. The accidental gunshot had tricked them into thinking he was somewhere else. Miss Quimby and Porfio could try to run the gap on their own. A fast run might get them through. It was a risk, but it was an even chance.

Meanwhile, he could go on over the slant and probably catch a mule, or even go back for ammunition for the peacemaker. Boggs was bound to have some somewhere on the coach. This was reason, and the rest was folly, but he remembered the bright glow that had come to Miss

Quimby's eyes when Doc had told her to take Porfio by the hand, and the answer she had given him, like deep quiet water. He had seen and heard something there that was far beyond the cynic's tongue, and whether Doc had outsmarted him or not had no bearing. He had to stand his ground, and, perhaps, go down when the last he had to offer was spent.

He stepped forward to the edge of the ledge and let out a yell. The Apaches spun and stared up. Ibsen stared back. He held them so, under his gun, nailed in their tracks with surprise and dismay. The gun hung limp in his hand. He didn't threaten them with it, but he held them, and he saw Porfio give a final boost and get Miss Quimby aboard, and he saw them start forward.

So long, the two Apaches stood frozen, but the clatter of hoofs brought a stir. They didn't actually move, but Ibsen saw the swift ripple of muscle brought to bear on some intended move. Like wolves on a hunt, they had an intuition for teamwork, and Ibsen thought he saw what they meant to do. The ledge on which they stood was wide, so they were obliged to stay near the edge to look down into the gap. The next terrace down was narrow and deep, so a man could get an unobstructed view of the gap and keep his back protected at the same time. One of them meant to go over the edge to block the two riders, the other meant to jump forward for cover and hold Ibsen off.

Vague straws, mere shadows of thought and intention, warned Ibsen. He raised his gun, and the two Apaches took off, one forward, the other backward, giving Ibsen a last hard choice, whether to fend for himself or the safety of the riders below. He made it fast, and the Apache going over the edge got it. He crumpled like a shot bird, and, from the sound, bounced down clear to the bottom. An avalanche of scree poured after him.

The other crouched behind the wall. Only the tip of his bow showed. Hot fury poured off his lips, but he kept to cover. The last of the smoke, the very last, trickled off Ibsen's gun. The weapon was useless now, no better than a stick, but he put it in his holster. Porfio looked up, and Ibsen waved, but he didn't get an answer. Either Porfio didn't see him or he was too busy keeping Miss Quimby aboard.

"There they go, Doc," Ibsen muttered, and with Doc's words thrown around them, they made a sight worth looking at. A part of all that was gone, of Deuce and Boggs and that Diogenes and even Watts, and much of Doc, and a little of himself, went with them. That bean-pole woman had it in her keeping, like seed to plant, and it would make a harvest, as surely as day came out of night.

The Apache below moved. He showed himself, and automatically Ibsen's hand went for his gun. The Apache ducked. His bow tip moved along the ledge. It moved clear out of sight, and, much later, Ibsen saw the Apache circling around the far side of the meadow. He was on the run. Ibsen didn't mind, but he was surprised, until he let it soak in that a gun wasn't entirely empty until the one it was pointed at knew it.

THE CAPTIVES

STEPHEN VINCENT BENÉT

It was good to have news of you, my dear Charles—you have no idea how eagerly we seize upon the mails from Britain, in this exile. Even a six-months-old scrap of gossip is chewed like a bone. I've no doubt the same is true of all foreign service, but here, in the colonies of America, you may take it for a fact. Indeed, sometimes I wonder whether it is truly the year of our Lord, 1764, or if I but doze and hibernate, as bears are said to do, in the wilderness.

My own budget will not repay yours, I fear. I cannot tell you of Lord X's duel with Lord Y, recount the witty things said by Mr. B at the coffeehouse, or how the world took Viscount Z's elopement to Gretna Green with the heiress. You question me as regards the late campaign, and, certainly, I shall do my best to inform you. To one who has played his part—and a noble one—in such a victory as that of Minden, our backwoods scufflings here must seem unworthy a true son of Mars. Nevertheless, there are certain details you will not find in the newsletters, and it is for these I crave your attention. To tell you the truth, this American campaign has unsettled my mind in a way I would not have believed possible, when we last spoke together. And the chief reason for that unsettlement has nothing to do with either strategy or tactics. Perhaps it is part of the vein of superstition that you have ever claimed, though pleasantly, was a part of my Scots' heritage. Yet I think we see things as clearly at Auchairn as you do in London, and perhaps with a deeper vision. Well, well, to my tale.

As you doubtless know, our difficulties at the outset of the business were grave enough—the war having broken out so suddenly and with such unexpected violence over the whole American frontier. I believe it to be generally thought, in England, that a few thousand whooping and painted savages are little to tax the strategy of a British general—and this after Braddock!—but, I assure you, it is not the case. No doubt they would be easy enough to deal with on the plains of the Low Countries, but here, in these loathsome and scarcely penetrable woods, it is a different affair. You smile a little—you have seen the forests of Germany. But these are not woods, they are wilder-

THE CAPTIVES

159

ness. The tree boughs meet above, the underbrush has never known the ax. At night there is a darkness of darkness and small, crying sounds. I despair of showing you the difference, yet it exists, like a creature that has not been tamed.

I joined the regiment in the West Indies, just in time to get my first dose of fever and sail for the Pennsylvania Colony with the effects still upon me. My Highlanders had been riddled by the disease—it was pitiful to see their plight. There were clansmen of mine in the regiment and they depended upon me, as men will—I fear ineffectually, for the most part. Indeed, I will confess to you that there was a moment when I did not see what use we might be in an active campaign, even granting that we reached the port of Philadelphia alive. But I did not know our new commander, Colonel Henry Bouquet.

A Swiss, a free sword of the old adventurous stripe and a most sagacious soldier—he had served under Forbes in the previous campaign and, in truth, did most of that business, Forbes being an old man and ailing. He is a red-faced man and careful of his dress, but you see the look of true command in his eyes. My Highlanders grinned woodenly when they heard that he was to lead them. For myself, I was perturbed at first, when I saw the exercises he put us to—for leaping over logs and darting from tree to tree are not part of the ordinary exercise of a soldier. There were those who thought it an undignified proceeding—they should try to cut their way through the wilderness at Pennsylvania. I can only say that my own men took to it like ducks to water—it was the way of fighting that we used at Preston Pans, if you will pardon the analogy.

Well, I will not rehearse the events of the war. We beat

the savages soundly at Bushy Run—they had thought to catch us there as they caught poor Braddock, but did not, thanks to our commander. A small affair, for Europe, but I may say, fiercely contested. It is incorrect to believe the savages will not stand fire—they charge with great dash and spirit. True, if you break them, they will run—so will any troops. You must fight them their own way, if you are to succeed—not by set volleys of musketry. L—d J—f—y A-h—st may be of a different opinion. I must say, and with no ill will, that I would L—d J—f—y had been at Bushy Run.

Well, we relieved Fort Pitt and, next year, pushed on to the Muskingum—it is a wide, flowing river. Now that is what I wish to talk about—you will think me daft for doing so, yet it weighs upon my mind. It was the question of the captives. Again, I despair of making you understand.

They had been captives for years, through all the Indian country. There were stolen girls who had grown to womanhood, there were men who had barely escaped the stake and the fire, there were children who had forgotten the sound of English speech. When we got to the Muskingum, the Indians began to bring them in. You have doubtless seen prisoners exchanged. This was not like that.

It was the season we call St. Martin's summer—a part of autumn when, for a week or two, the warmth and the light of summer return, before the snow. They call it Indian summer here, and it is a most beautiful time. More beautiful than in England, for the sky seems made of blue smoke and the trees turn bright red and gold. It is dauntingly beautiful, yet there is something fey about it. You would not think that a wilderness could look so fair and so

peaceful. And yet the gold is fairy gold, and might vanish
at a touch.

Now had we been but invaders—and, indeed, there were
times when I felt strange enough—all might have been ac-
cording to rule. But with us were the Virginia and Pennsylvania riflemen—and, many of them, come for that thing
alone. It was their own blood and their own kin they sought
to recover, not ours. That makes a difference. I shall try to
describe them to you. They wear linsey shirts and leather
breeches; they are tall, strong men. They are not rich in
possessions, yet they do not look like hinds or yeomen.
They carry their rifles lightly and they walk with a long,
springing step. You would know the likeness—you, who
have seen our poor, proud clansmen in the Highlands. But
these are Germans, Irish, English—God knows what they
are, yet all walk the same and carry their heads high. I
could understand it, at Auchairn—after all, we are all of
the same stock there, and we cleave to the chief. But they
have no chief and yet they have the pride. There is no
one man among them who does not feel himself a man and
the equal of any. They are difficult to command—yet I
have seen them drive the head of a nail with a bullet at
fifty yards. To be sure, they are both rough and rustic—
it is a rough life they lead. Yet, somehow it is their country,
rather than ours—I can put it no other way, and yet I
know you will smile and ask me what I mean.

I had speech with a number of them—they are laconic
but humorous. They were not always respectful of the
prowess of British arms, but they liked Bouquet. Most of
all they were anxious for the captives—I shall tell you of
that.

When the first eighteen were brought in by the Delawares, I felt very appropriate sentiments, I can tell you. A pitiful troop they seemed, clad in skins like the savages themselves and so burned by the sun as hardly to be distinguished from them. It was shocking to me to see those of my own kind and race reduced to such a condition. I expected to see anguish and horror writ clear upon every face. And yet, when the thing was accomplished—and it was not till after a deal of ceremonious speechmaking—I saw a young, tow-headed Virginia rifleman step up to one of the wild figures.

"Well, Henry," he said with a drawl—they slur their speech in a manner I cannot reproduce—"you've kind of filled out in the brisket. But you're looking peart, at that."

"Thanks, Tom," said the strange, wild figure in the same accent. "I reckoned if they sent a war party, you'd be with it. Obliged to you. Say, have you got any Christian tobacco? I been smoking willow bark all winter. Wasn't bad, excepting for that."

Then the two brothers beat each other upon the back, whooping and swearing strange oaths that I did not comprehend. A tall, painted savage watched them; it seemed to me, scornfully. After a moment the brother who had been a captive, turned.

"Oh, Tom," he said, indicating the savage, "this here's Little Bear. He's a friend of mine. His ma 'dopted me. Guess if she hadn't, they'd have burned me—they seemed to be fixing to. But him and the old lady stood up for me something handsome. Treated me right. Like you two to be acquainted."

"That so?" said the other brother. He raised his hand

and made a sign—it was odd to see a white man do it with
the slow dignity of a savage.

"What's their word for peace?" he said.

The other brother gave it and he repeated it. Not a
muscle seemed to change in the savage's countenance but
now he, too, made a sign and began to speak.

"He's saying you're my brother so he's your brother,"
said Henry. "But you ain't to believe all he says—I helped
him out in a pinch once, but why wouldn't I?" His tone was
precisely the tone of an anxious collegian, introducing some
new-found friend. "Where's that tobacco of yours? We'd
better have a smoke on it. Say, that's fine."

It was then I began to understand a little of what goes
on in these wildernesses. The man, Henry, was younger
than I, yet to him captivity and rescue were part of the nor-
mal lot of life. That would be comprehensible in a soldier,
but he was not a soldier. At the end, there was a ceremonious leave-taking between himself and Little Bear. Yet,
when I had speech with him later, he talked to me as cheerfully of killing Indians as a man might of knocking over a
hare. There was no inconsistency to it—he could not imagine a life lived another way.

I shall not describe all that I saw—it would take a better
pen than mine. I have seen a woman dressed in skins give
a wild high cry and run to the husband who had thought
her lost forever. I have seen a woman from the pack trains
go endlessly up and down through the throng of captives,
muttering, "A little boy named Jamie Wilson. Has anybody seen a little boy named Jamie Wilson? He wore a
blue cap and is about ten years old." I have seen memory
and recognition come back into a child's eyes, when, at

first, he strained away from the strange, white faces and would have gone back to his savage foster kin. There were women who had red husbands and red children. They were delivered over to us faithfully, loaded with the poor gifts of the woods, yet, before we had reached Fort Pitt, there were some who had slipped away and back to the bark lodges. We did our best to retain them—indeed, we bound one or two, though I thought that wrong—but the forest had entered into their veins, and they would not stay. I shall tell you of one other woman and then my tale will have an end.

It was part of my duties to help make out a muster roll of the rescued—and that is how I first saw her. She had come in with a group from the villages of the Shawnees, but, though with them, she was not of them—she always stood a little apart. That is how I shall always think of her— a little apart from the rest. A gray-eyed girl, slight but strong, with hair that the sun had bleached to a silvery gold. She was dressed, like the others, in the gear of the savage, and there was an old Indian woman with her who made much of her and howled when she was taken away. She was perfectly biddable and quiet, but none appeared to claim her from among our men and women. Well, there were others in that case, and yet, somehow, she was different. There are wild legends of women turned into deer. I could believe them, looking at her face.

When there was an opportunity, I questioned her, though the opportunity did not come till the evening. I then saw that she was younger than I had imagined—indeed, she could not have been more than sixteen. She answered my questions pleasantly and with dignity, though there was little she could tell. She had been captured, as I gathered, somewhere in Western Pennsylvania and she knew her name to be Mary. But of what her last name had been she had no recollection, though, she assured me, she had often tried to recall it. The cabin had been beside a stream, but to each name of a river that I mentioned she gravely shook her head. It was always called the river, to her remembrance—she could tell me no more.

No, she could not remember neighbors, but her father had worn a beard and her mother had had a red apron. There had been a little brother—she remembered the look of him very well. Then, one day, she had strayed into the woods, got lost, and fallen asleep. As she told it to me, gravely and sweetly, in her halting English, it was like one of our own old rude ballads of children stolen away to dwell in a green hill. For that was the last she saw of hearth and home. There were scalps at the belts of the raiding party that found her—she thought one to be her mother's by the color and texture of the hair, but she was not sure. This she told me with the unstudied, poignant matter-of-factness of a child. I gather, at the time, she must have been about six years old.

Why the Shawnees had spared her instead of dispatching her I cannot tell—it is a thing that happens at times. Since then she had lived with them, not unhappily. From time to time she had seen other captives—so kept her English. There had been, in particular, a woman named Margaret McMurtrie, a later captive, and kind to her. She had tried to teach her something of white ways, though they did not always sound very comfortable. And now, after all of this, she was going back to a white world.

It may not seem logical, but I cannot tell you how forcible an impression her recital made upon me. It was not only the

story but the circumstances—the girl's clear, candid face in
the red light of the campfire—the great sky above us with
its stars. I wondered privately to myself why she, unlike so
many others, had no Indian husband. Then, looking at her,
suddenly I knew. There was a fey quality to her—an un-
awakened simplicity. I queried her.

"Yes," she said in her careful English, "they thought I
helped with the corn. It is very important to have the corn
good. They did not wish to give me a husband till they were
sure the corn would like it. Perhaps they will take me back
again, but I do not think so. You are very strong people,
you English."

"I am Scots," I said, "not English. But you are English."

"Am I?" she said. "Well then, I suppose I am. But I do
not know what I am." And she smiled at the fire.

"And what do you think of me—of us—now you have
found us?" I said, with a man's blundering.

She looked me over gravely and candidly. "Why, I think
you wear very pretty clothes," said she, touching my sleeve
with a child's inquisitiveness. "You must have wonderful
animals to give you clothes like that."

That was how we talked together at first—and yet, how
might I have done otherwise? I wish you would tell me. It
was part of my duty to make out the rolls—part of my duty
to assist the captives. The child could not remember ever
having seen a wheeled vehicle before she came to our
camp. Would you think I could play the schoolteacher?
I would not have thought so myself. Yet I taught her the
greater part of her letters, on our way to Fort Pitt and beyond it, and she proved an obedient scholar. You will say
it is the Scotsman in me, yet you would have done the
same. I could not bear to think of her as merely childish

or a savage, when she looked at me out of her gray eyes. The Bible, fortunately, she knew of—her father had been wont to read a chapter of it aloud in the evenings, and that good woman, Margaret McMurtrie, had been a professing Christian. We used to read a chapter of it aloud, by the campfire, and I would expound it to her as best I might. Now and then I would hit upon some verse that touched a chord of memory and a puzzled, rapt expression would come upon her face.

You see it was my thought—God knows why—that if, by any means, I could make her remember her name and more of her past history than she knew, the spell of the wilderness might be shaken from her. I do not know why I thought so—and, indeed, it will seem to you a matter of little import. What matter if she lived and died, unlettered and savage? There are many such, in the wilderness. And yet, it mattered to me. I knew how a man must feel whose bride has been, as we say, fairy-kist, and comes back to him out of the green hill, but not as she went away. Yet I did my best—you will laugh to hear what I did. By the time we had passed Fort Pitt, she could say the first half of her catechism very fairly. Yet, if I must be honest, it did not seem to me that she spoke with understanding. She would repeat her answers as well as any lass, but I could not feel that grace had penetrated her heart. Yet it was not a hard heart, or a recalcitrant, as I should know.

The belief of the Indians is not easy to set down, yet, at the core, it is simple. They are not blind idolaters, like the pagans of old, and they worship a spirit of presence, though they name him differently. At least, that is what she told me. I should be glad to think she told me truly. It is hideous to think of whole nations consigned from birth to the pit or the flame, though John Calvin makes no bones of it. Yet she must have been baptized a Christian, even if she could not remember it. I kept cleaving to that.

I remember one night when we were talking, and she told me of the devils in tree and water that her friends also believed in. At least they seemed like devils to me, though perhaps they were not. I could not bear to hear her and I groaned aloud.

"Why, what is the matter? Are you sick?" she said, with her candid stare at me and the light on her silver-gold hair.

"No, not sick," I said.

"If you are sick," she said, "why, that's easy, for a man. You will go to the sweat lodge and feel better. But, I forget—you English do not use the sweat lodge."

"Child," I said, very gently, "will a time never come when you say 'we English' instead?"

"I try to say that," she said. "But I forget." It maddened me, for some reason, to hear her say so without fear or shame.

"Woman," I cried, like any dominie, "have you no fear of God's judgments? Do you not see that every day you have spent in the wilderness has been a day without grace?"

"I do not know what you mean," she said. "Sometimes the sun shines and sometimes the snow falls. In the winter, we often go hungry but, in the spring, the hunters kill game again. And even in winter, there is much to do—the fire to be tended, the deerskins to be chewed and made soft."

"God gave you an immortal soul," I said. "Have you no feeling for it?"

She looked at me with her fey look—the look of a change-ling.

"Now you talk like a medicine man," she said. She sighed. "They are very terrible and wonderful, of course. But a woman has other business."

"In God's name, what?" I said.

She opened her eyes wide. "Why," she said, "to know how to work the skins and cook the food—yes, and plant the corn and the beans. You think that is hard work—but the Englishwomen I have talked to who come from the towns have harder. They live shut up in their towns like corn shut up in a pouch, and they wear so many clothes the air never gets to their skin. They say it is a noble life, but I do not see how they bear it. We are often cold and hungry, but when there is food we share it, and there is always the sky above and the earth beneath."

"But what is the end of it all?" I said, for it seemed to me she talked like a pagan or a child.

"Oh," she said, "go to a man's lodge and lie by his side and bear his children. That is the end of it all."

"Would you have done that?" I said.

"Why, yes," she said. "Next year, perhaps. Not this year, for they were not sure of the corn." She flushed, faintly. "He was a strong man, though older," she said. "He had plenty in his lodge and he killed many enemies."

The thought of it made me desperate. "I do not understand women," I said in a groaning voice. "I think I do not understand them at all."

I rose and walked up and down in front of the fire.

"Why are you walking up and down?" she said in an interested voice. "Are you thinking of your own enemies? Be content—I am sure you will kill many of them. You are strong and quick."

"No, child, no." I said. "I am thinking of your soul and

my soul and—" I stopped and sat down beside her again.

"There is an old song," I said. "It is sung in my country of a man who was led astray. I do not know why I wish to sing it to you, but I wish it."

So sitting beside her, by the campfire, in the great woods, I sang her the rough old ballad of Thomas the Rhymer, or as much as I could remember—how he met the Queen of Elfland and she took him where man should not go.

> "Now ye maun go wi' me," she said
> "True Thomas, ye maun go wi' me;
> And ye maun serve me seven years,
> Thro' weal or woe as chance may be."

I sang, and wondered, as I sang, if it were the eildron tree that, in truth, we sat beneath—the tree that is on the border of another land than ours. But when I reached the verse that says,

> It was mirk, mirk night, there was nae starlight,
> They waded through red bluid to the knee,

she nodded her head, and when I ended the song, she nodded again.

"That is a fine song," she said. "There is strong medicine in it. He was a strong chief—yet he did not have to go with her unless he wished it. It is so in some of our stories."

I could not speak, but sat watching her. There was an intent and puzzled look upon her face. It seemed to me that I saw her from a great distance.

"There is something in the song," she said. "I cannot remember." She put her hand to her head. "I cannot remember," she said again. "But there was something in the song. I have heard it and another—another. The queen was not clad in green—she was clad in scarlet. Do you know of that?"

She looked at me pitifully and eagerly, while her brows knitted, but I did not know how to help her. She struck her hands together and sang:

> The Queen was clad in scarlet
> Her merry maids all in green,

"Eh, feyther, I ken the tune—I will not fail you."

I joined her in a low voice, greatly daring, but I do not know that she heard me, her face was so rapt and content.

"Ride hooly, hooly gentlemen," she sang, "ride hooly now wi' me."

Then, for a moment, her voice stumbled and faltered but only to come strongly and piercingly on the verse all Scotland knows.

> Yestreen the Queen had four Maries,
> The night she'll hae but three;
> There was Marie Seaton and Marie Beaton
> And Marie Carmichael and me.

Then she gave a great loud cry. "Carmichael—Mary Carmichael!" she said. "Hide yourself in the cupboard by the door, Jamie—the Indians are coming and feyther's head is all red!" And with the cry, her voice broke and she burst into a passion of tears. I held her in my arms, scarcely daring to breathe till it had passed, for I knew that with that, name and recollection and Christian memory had come back to her.

Well, that is the wilderness tale I have to tell you—a strange one enough, I think, though with no true sequel. I have talked since with a medical man in Philadelphia of much experience—he deems it probable that the sound of the Scots' words and the lilt of the tune touched some hidden spring in the girl's mind and she knew, having long forgotten, that she was Mary Carmichael. It must have been a song that her father sang her oft.

I know myself that, from that moment, there was a certain change in her, though I did not perceive it till afterward. For the next day I fell ill of my fever again, and they tell me I was skin and bones when they brought me in to Carlisle.

When I came to myself again, and that was not for more days than I care to count, she was sitting by my bedside. I could not account for the difference in her at first—then I saw she was decently dressed in Christian homespun, no longer in the gear of the savage. I should have rejoiced to see that and yet I did not.

"You were singing, but I cannot remember the tune," I said, for those were the first words that came into my head.

"Hush," she said, and smoothed my coverlet with her hand like any woman. "You have been very sick. You must rest awhile."

After I had grown stronger, I found from the woman in whose house I lay that she, Mary Carmichael, had come each day to nurse me. Also she had prepared certain draughts of leaves and herbs. I cannot remember drinking them, but I fear they have entered forever into my veins.

She was not too changed, you understand. Even in the sad dress of the frontier, there was still a strangeness about her. But the changeling look had gone. She was very calm and kindly, sitting by my bedside, yet I knew I could not keep her or hold her, though I would dream at night of bringing her back to Auchairn.

When I was quite strong again and she brought in the man named Henry—the strong, yellow-haired youth whose friend had been Little Bear—I knew that that, too, was fitting. They were of a likeness and I was not of their likeness. When I had the barber in to powder my hair, I knew there was no likeness between us.

They were to be married next day, and they asked me to stand up with them, so I did so. The church, as it happened, was full, for the wedding of a captive caused great interest in the town. It is a plain, small church, but the minister was of the right persuasion.

Before that she thanked me very sweetly and civilly for teaching her her letters and for all that I had done. It was hard to bear, to have her thank me, yet now I am glad she did, for I shall remember it. The man thanked me also and wrung my hand. It was odd—he was shyer than she, in the church, though I had seen him friendly enough on the march. He had his rifle, his ax, and a pack horse with some goods upon it. They were going to a place called the Forks of the Yadkin—it is many miles away in the rougher part of Virginia. From there, he thought, they might venture some day to the wilds of a new land called Ken-tuck-e—a land full of game and grass where few white men had ever trod. It was odd to stand beside that man and, though one day I will be Auchairn, to feel myself poor beside him. Yet I have a good conceit of myself, as a rule.

The minister—a good man—made them an excellent and searching discourse on Christian wedlock. She listened to it attentively, but I have certain fears that she would have listened quite as prettily to the heathenish ravings of a medicine man. Then they set off together, he and she. The last glimpse I had was of the silvery hair, as they topped the rise and began to go down. It was a clear day, not yet cold. He had his rifle in the crook of his arm—she walked a little behind him, leading the pack horse. She did not walk like a lady, but freely, and you could not hear her steps, though the ground was covered with blown leaves.

The adventure has left me confused—I thought it might help my confusion to write it down. You will say it is all simple enough—that I fell in love with a rustic beauty for a few weeks, behaved like a gentleman and a Christian, and was glad to see her married off, in the end. That is true, perhaps, and yet there is something more. Even now, I cannot get the thought of those two people out of my mind. By now, no doubt, they will have reached the Forks of the Yadkin, and he will be making his clearing—there, in the utter wilderness that to them is home. It is there that their children will be born—or in some even wilder land. Yet was she very much of a woman, when she took me by the sleeve and said I wore pretty clothes.

They are not English or Scots—they are not German or Irish—it is a new nation they are making. We are deceived by the language, and even that begins to change on their tongues. Oh yes, I have been graciously received in fine houses in Philadelphia, but that was an imitation, as Bath is a little London. It is different, in the wilderness—and our Lords in Council have not fathomed it. As for me, I have taken the king's shilling, and some day I shall be Auchairn. Yet were it not so—I swear I should like to see what children came of such a marriage. Aye, even did it mean the abandonment of all I have been.

You will think me daft to have such thoughts in my head —it may be I am not yet wholly recovered of the fever. It may also be that I shall never recover. We hear that the government intends to close the western frontiers to settlement—no doubt for good reasons of policy. But these people are not to be stayed, and I have seen them fight. Had they a Bouquet to lead them—well, this is all speculation. Yet I still keep thinking of my changeling. Aye, even had all things been otherwise, I could not have brought her back tamed, to be lady of Auchairn. And yet, she had nations in her eyes.

PONY-EXPRESS BOY

M. G. CHUTE

Even in his sleep, Joby remembered that this was the day. He rolled over on his blanket and tried to wake up with a quiet, manly grunt. But it didn't work. He was sitting up before even his eyes were open, and it was hard to keep from bursting out with a good big whoop. That was how fine he felt.

From this day forward he was an expressman with a regular beat. From this day forward his pay was better than doubled, and he was a man with a big job and a big future. Maybe in thirty or forty years he'd be president of the company; the way folks talked about California, chances were there'd always be a need for fast letter service between Saint Joe and San Francisco. Likely that was how Alice was figuring things this morning, too. Alice would like being the wife of the company president. Rigged out in blue with lace cuddling up under her chin, she'd be prettier than any girl in the whole of Saint Joe or San Francisco, or New York or Paris for that matter.

Joby opened his eyes and took a sterner grip on himself. Daydreaming was for kids and women. A man dealt with facts only and the day's work. Joby took a deep breath, but the facts weren't much of a help, either, toward sobering him down. Before the afternoon was well started, he'd be at the end of his run, and out from the home station would come Gus Webb and Mrs. Gus and Alice, their eyes bulging and excited on account of the record time he had made. And when Will had gone on with the mail, and Gus and Mrs. Gus, out of politeness, had gone back into the house, then Alice would come up to him, smiling and proud, and she would say, "Joby, you done well," and after that he could kiss her hard and long on the mouth.

That was how Gus and Mrs. Gus had promised. "Wait until you're older or until you get a man's job," they had told him. And he had a man's job now. Even Gus would figure there weren't many fellows starting to hold down jobs as expressmen at seventeen.

Suddenly there wasn't any way he could keep calm any longer. "Whee!" said Joby. "Ai-yi-yi-yi-eee!"

Across the room, cooking breakfast at the fireplace, Tex turned around on his heels. "Breakfast's ready," said Tex, "if you ain't planning to ride with your stomach as empty as your brains."

"Yes, sir," said Joby. He pulled on his boots, stuffing his trousers' legs down into their tops. Tex was a big man with a voice that was always low-down and gloomy-sounding. "Yes, sir," Joby repeated, making his voice manly sounding too.

Tex rubbed his arms across the table, which was an empty candle box tipped over on its side. Then he put a plateful of flapjacks down on the box. "Dooley," Tex said, "is a sitting out with 'Relia."

"Oh." Joby, ashamed, let the six flapjacks he had picked up drop back down on the plate. In his excitement over its being the morning, he had forgotten about Mr. Dooley's poor cow. "How's she feeling?"

"Sickening fast. Reckon she'll go under with the sun today."

Joby said, "Oh," again. He felt that the approaching end of Aurelia required some comment, but he couldn't get his mind long enough off the delicate brownness of the flapjacks to think up one. Maybe taking fewer flapjacks at a time would be the respectful method under the circumstances.

Tex poured coffee into a pint tin cup and put it down next to the plate. "Way I look at it is, ain't cow meat as good for man as cow milk?"

"Sure," said Joby, "if he'll let her be et." He laid one flapjack in the palm of his left hand, arranged strips of bacon across its surface, poured molasses on the whole, and then, with a single flip, before the molasses had time to run off, neatly rolled everything up together. Even in the presence of the cow's last illness, a man had to eat.

Tex watched while Joby repeated the process with the next five flapjacks. Then he sighed heavily. "Men or cows, it's all the same. If they live through the dust and the heat, the alkali in the water will get 'em. Land ain't fit for cows, let alone Christians, to get buried in."

Thickly, through flapjacks and molasses, Joby murmured with convincing somberness, "It's plain hell all right."

Tex nodded and went outside to do the saddling. Left alone, Joby folded the remaining flapjacks and bacon into one large, firm roll, and worked it by installments into his mouth. While he ate, he tried to keep his mind sobered by being sorry for the station keeper, who had sat up all night with Aurelia. He was a man now with a man's job, and only kids went whooping around like brainless coyotes.

Joby licked some of the stickiness from his hands and went and got his revolver and hat. Then he sawed off six pieces of bread and hacked off three pieces of cold meat, and put them together with nice plasterings of bacon grease that was just beginning to harden. Before going outside he stowed the sandwiches away in various parts of the clothing he was wearing.

The pony Tex had saddled was a dainty little mare less than fourteen hands high, but there wasn't an ounce of politeness in her. She hadn't kicked anybody's head off yet, but she was still trying, hopeful and eager.

Joby stood with one hand on her headstall, the other gentling her about the neck. Her name was Sweet Lady, and she had more real bottom than any horse Joby had ever seen. McGuire, who'd had the run up until today, hadn't liked Sweet Lady, but Joby was lighter than McGuire. Joby, even with twenty flapjacks inside himself, weighed less than a hundred and twenty pounds. With

Joby on her back, Sweet Lady couldn't help but make a record.

Tex kept his head turned toward the west, waiting for sight or sound of Charley and the eastbound express. "Bet you," said Tex, "he'll be late."

"Maybe," said Joby. From this day forward he was a real rider. Once near Fort Kearney he had pinch-hit on a short ride for a fellow who'd got himself a bad cold, but this was different. Now he was the man who had the run between Dooley's ranch and Gus Webb's station, and nobody had it but him. To keep from suffocating, Joby took a big, deep breath.

"I'll bet you—" said Tex. "Say, that's him, ain't it?"

Joby watched the cloud of dust and when, after a long time, it was still holding close to the ground instead of scooting off as a little whirlwind, he nodded and took a firmer hold on the pony's bridle. It was wonderful how, standing with her back to the west, Sweet Lady could know that the mail for the east was coming in, and get fidgety for the start.

"Quit it!" Joby said happily.

After that it was Joby who did most of the fidgeting, but he couldn't help it. Mr. Dooley was so slow leaving Aurelia's side that Tex had the leather cover, which held the mail, off Charley's horse and on to Joby's before the station keeper got there.

Charley staggered slightly when he got to the ground, and Tex looked at him anxiously. "Listen, Charley, you ain't sick, too, are you? We got 'Relia crippled up, and—"

Charley gave a short laugh. "I'd sure enjoy seeing how you felt after riding seventy miles on a supper of pickled oysters and beans."

Mr. Dooley had finally got the little brass padlock off the front left pocket that held the way mail and the waybill, but he was looking carefully at all the letters, reading the names aloud, as though there was surely some mail meant for his station.

Tex said, "A grown fellow should know better'n to ride on pickled oysters."

"Ha!" said Charley. "Listen, by the time the supply wagons get past you, there's nothing left for any stations west of here but pickled oysters. Nary a drop of whisky, nary a lump of sugar! What a life we got!"

"Hush!" Tex said very loudly. Then he jerked a thumb in the direction of Joby. "The kid's dreaming he's in heaven. What you want to do—wake him up?"

Joby's face got red; he could feel the color running out clear to the tips of his ears. But then Sweet Lady gave a jerk, and excitement and happiness got back into Joby.

"Look, Mr. Dooley, ain't it time I got started?"

Mr. Dooley wrapped the letters carefully back in their oiled-silk covering. Then he got out his watch and began work on the waybill card. "We're ahead of schedule, boy. Just you try and rest easy."

Writing down the time of arrival and the time of leaving was the last part of the business that had to be got through. Joby took a tighter hold on the saddlebow, and the second Mr. Dooley pinched the padlock shut, Joby jumped.

The pony whirled in a complete circle, then, facing east once more, broke into a run. Joby straightened slightly in his saddle and gave a loud whoop.

"Go it, Lady!" Joby yelled excitedly. He had sixty-eight miles to ride, and five ponies on which to ride them, and if the other ponies were even half as good as the one he

was on, he couldn't help but make a record. He'd arrive at
Gus Webb's station so far ahead of schedule that Will
wouldn't even be ready to ride.

"Yi-yi-yi!" Joby howled. Then, because the sun and the
wind were both coming straight at him, he pulled the brim
of his hat farther down over his face. Two of his fingers
came through the brim, and he had a time getting them
loose again. When he got to Gus Webb's place, Alice would
want to mend it for him. She would maybe want to em-
broider the holes up with beads. And maybe he would let
her. Or maybe he would say no, because a man getting paid
a hundred dollars a month had money enough to buy himself a new hat.

What he would do would be to pretend he was planning
to buy a new hat, planning to buy a whole new outfit with
fancy leggings and silver-plated spurs. And when he'd
teased her plenty, then he'd give her the hat to mend, and
she'd know for sure that his plans were to save all his pay
for getting married on. First her eyes would get big and
solemn, and then slowly her mouth would begin to smile,
from the corners in.

He'd have two whole days with Alice before Will returned with the westbound mail. And Mr. and Mrs. Gus
would leave them alone a lot of the time. Even when he
had been nothing but an extra boy, getting sent around
from station to station, sometimes to help the blacksmith,
sometimes to bullwhack with the company's supply train
when a regular driver got to ailing, even then Gus and Mrs.
Gus had thought it was all right for him to be liking their
daughter.

And he'd show them it was all right, too. He was an expressman now at a hundred a month, and the first run he

made would be a record run. After that, there wasn't any telling how soon he'd be a division agent.

Because of the pleasantness of his thoughts, it seemed to Joby as though only a few seconds had gone by before he was in sight of the first way station and his first twelve-mile stretch was over. In front of the station a horse and a man stood in readiness.

Joby leaned forward in his saddle. "Go it, Lady!" he croaked. The dust in his throat made the croak, but Sweet Lady understood all right.

With one hand Joby loosened the leather covering from his saddletree. Then he raised himself slightly in his stirrups and jerked the mail sacks out from under his legs.

He gave a whoop for a warning. Then he tossed the sacks ahead, so that they landed almost squarely at the station keeper's feet and were picked up and adjusted to the fresh pony's back before Joby's horse came to a stop.

Joby jumped off the near side of Sweet Lady and on the off side of the horse the man was holding. The fresh horse reared, and Joby waved his hand, dug in his heels, and yelled, "All's well along the road!"

That hadn't taken more than ten seconds. But it could have taken less. With a little leap he could have made the change without touching a foot to the ground. There weren't many riders who could do that, most of them being either too heavy or too slow. But, properly done, it would save whole seconds.

The new horse was a pinto, a little larger than Sweet Lady, but when it settled down to an even run, it had a nice, easy stride that covered the ground.

"Horse," said Joby, "you're heading for a record!"

Right from the beginning Alice had known that Joby

would make good. But even she wouldn't be expecting that his first run would be a record. She'd been excited and pleased enough when she'd heard that he'd got the job. Last week, when word had come from the agent at Carson City that Joby would have McGuire's run, McGuire wanting to head for the mines again, Joby had given McGuire a letter to carry to her on his last run. McGuire had carried it in the band of his hat, and when he got back, he told Joby that Alice had sure looked pleased— "got red as a tasty young lobster, she did."

She was pretty, Alice was. She was the prettiest girl west of the Mississippi; maybe east of it, too, but Joby couldn't more than guess about that, never having been east of it. She had hair smooth and pretty like molasses, and her eyes were large and soft like a little calf's, and her hands were cool as— There wasn't anything in the desert that was like them; a fellow had to close his eyes and think about rose petals and violet flowers to get even near to what they were like. And in only a few hours he would be seeing her and she would be saying, "Joby, you done well." And then he could kiss her.

"Yi-yi-yi!" Joby yelped.

The station keeper, holding the next horse in readiness, yipped back and grabbed the sacks that Joby threw. Close alongside of the fresh horse, Joby reined in. Then he gave a sideways leap.

For a minute, thinking that his heart was going to pump its way out of his chest and that he was going to die, Joby sat on the ground with his eyes closed.

When he opened his eyes, he felt even more terrible. The two horses had twisted their heads around and were looking down at him. And the station keeper was looking down at him, too.

"I reckon, kid," the station keeper said, "you best rest up a bit 'fore you get onto Baby. Takes a bit of seasoning to ride hard and fast like you done."

Joby rolled over and got up, thinking fast. "There, I figure that's enough," he said briskly. He gave a pat to the seat of his pants. "Getting dust on 'em holds 'em tighter to the saddle. Like spitting on your hands before you take hold of a spade." The station keeper looked like he was getting ready to laugh. "Well, it does!" said Joby, and climbed up fast as he could onto Baby's back.

Behind him Joby heard the man calling after him something about Indians, but he didn't wait to be insulted any more. Inside of a week every station between Carson City and Salt Lake would have heard how he'd sat down on dust instead of leather.

For a couple of minutes Joby was very sorry for himself, but then he began to think about Alice again and the record he was making. It would take a lot of falls from saddles before he would be behind schedule.

"Move along, Baby!" Joby begged anxiously.

And also he had Baby's light ways to deal with. She kept seeing her own private mirages, things like rattlesnakes that reared up under her nose and jack rabbits that she dreamed were trying to run between her legs. And, besides that, there was his own hunger to occupy his mind.

The sun wasn't straight overhead yet, but Joby's stomach didn't go by any clock. The sandwiches he had made were wonderful in their firmness. The bacon grease had hardened, fastening the meat slabs so well together that even

Baby's leaps couldn't jar them loose. Joby ate with deep appreciation.

At the end of the fourteen-mile run, he could see that what had happened to him might have happened to any man. It was merely that he had been trying to save time and had used the wrong method. In front of the new station Joby gave a lusty whoop, but he got down carefully from Baby's back and planted both feet firmly on the ground before he raised himself onto the back of the fresh horse.

"Howdy and 'by!" Joby yelled. But the station keeper and his assistant clung to the bridle of the fresh horse until they had had their say, which was that Joby was to tell the first company supply wagon that came through from Salt Lake City that they had better come prepared to dig two graves.

"Indians came last night. Took ten pounds of flour and all the bacon! Sneaked 'em while our backs was turned! Took the 'baccy too. Took every blame thing that stands between us and—"

"Listen, kid," the taller man said, "if you've got a crumb of brains, you'll quit like McGuire quit. There's only two ways to die out here. Either you starve to death or you burn to death, and neither is pleasant. . . . Hey, watch out!"

The pressure from Joby's heels had only been light, but the horse must have been scared, too, that the gentleman and his assistant would never stop talking, because it reared up on its hind legs like a bullet had clipped past its nose.

Joby said "Oof!" loudly, to show that he, too, had been surprised. Then he leaned forward a little on the horse's neck, and he was riding fast, and everything was fine again.

Joby had been sorry for the two men, but only just politely sorry, because both of them had been taking bites of tobacco in a kind of grand and easy style that showed there was more where those chunks had come from. And anybody that complained about the weather was just a natural-born complainer and didn't deserve much sympathy.

Maybe it was hot, but it was good desert heat that dried you off before you even got wet from it. And if God hadn't thought it was an all-right place for folks to live in, He wouldn't have put California on its other side.

"Ain't that so, horse?" said Joby.

And it was good land too. With more water it might even, Joby figured, grow things. As it was, it made a grand roadbed for fast-running horses. It was a beautiful land, and it had Alice living in it.

When Joby hit the station at the Springs, the last way stop before Gus Webb's home station, his throat was so dry that he couldn't give a really loud whoop. But the station keeper had heard hoofbeats and was out in the yard.

Joby waved his hand, threw the saddle sack ahead, and slid down on his feet. The old man, who was the station keeper, had a tin cup of cold coffee in his hand, but he was standing alone without any horse. Joby took a gulp out of the cup, licked his lips, and grabbed hold of the old man's arm.

"Look, I'm early, ain't I?"

"Yep."

"Well, look, I want to make a record." When the old man didn't move, Joby shook his arm excitedly.

"You're supposed to have a horse ready for me, ain't you?"

"Killed my dog, the Injuns did. Killed my Lassie."

"I—I'm sorry," said Joby. "I'm sorry 'bout your dog, but I want a horse quick, see?"

"Killed my Lassie with an arrow through her head."

"That was a mean trick," said Joby. He put the cup into one of the old man's hands and the reins of the tired horse into his other. "You wait here."

Joby ran around to the back end of the abode building to the part that was the stables. In front of the door was Lassie, still with the arrow sticking out of her head. Joby stepped over her and into the half darkness.

There was space for four horses, but there wasn't a horse around. Joby ran down one side of the stables and back up the other side. Then he ran through the one room of the house and out the front door.

"Injuns run off with all of 'em?" Joby yelled.

"Killed my Lassie too," said the old man. He watched while Joby slung the mail sack back on the tired pony, but he didn't make a move to help.

When he was up on the pony, Joby reached down and took the reins from the old man's hand. "Company wagons are due here inside of two days, but I'll tell Gus Webb how things are with you, and maybe something can be done sooner."

There wasn't anything that could be done sooner, but two days was a long time for a fellow to have to wait, unless he had hopes of something happening between times. Past the Springs, Joby turned in his saddle to wave his hand back to the old man, but the old man had already gone into his house.

Joby was sorry for the old man, but he was sorrier for the horse he was on. It was cows like Aurelia and ponies like this one that had all the really bad luck. Fourteen miles at top speed was about all a horse could stand with any pleasure. Another twelve miles was going to seem pretty hard on the animal.

"You got Injuns to blame for your troubles, horse," Joby said.

Then he leaned away forward in the saddle, keeping his weight as much as he could off the pony's hindquarters. And for almost the whole of the twelve miles he talked to the little horse, telling it about how grandly it was doing, and about how good water would feel on a dry throat and grain on an empty stomach, and about how, probably, there wasn't another pony between there and the ocean could equal its speed.

During the time that he wasn't talking to the pony, Joby tried singing to it. But the horse ran better to the talking, and so mostly he talked, keeping his voice low and persuasive.

The horse had maybe lost some of its enthusiasm, but, for most of the way, it went at a full gallop. It took more than Indian tricks to keep the company mail from making records when it was carried by some folks that Joby could name.

"Yi-yi-yi!" Joby howled happily. Then he reached up with one hand and wiped some of the dust off his face. He was in sight of the home station, and in a few minutes he would be seeing Alice. "Say, call this a record?" said Joby aloud. "You wait and see what I can do next time, when all my horses are fresh!"

There was nobody in the station yard, and that must mean that he was well over half an hour ahead of when they were expecting him. Maybe a long time ahead. He was good, he was.

Once in the station yard, Joby added a screech and a coyote yelp to his whoopings, but the door was tight-closed and stayed that way. For a second Joby got to thinking about Indians, but such foolishness only lasted a second. Then he pulled in his horse and got down.

"Oh-h-h Alice! Gus! Will!" Joby hollered. "Ah-o-o-o!"

He drew the reins down over the horse's head and started around the corner of the house.

"Howdy," said Gus Webb.

Joby pulled the pony up next to the station keeper. "Listen, Gus, I sort of figure I made a record getting here."

He watched anxiously while Gus opened the padlock to the front left pocket, looked at his watch, then wrote on the waybill.

"Did I?" said Joby.

"Did you what?" said Gus.

"Did I make a record?"

"Oh, sure, I reckon. Joby, you go eat."

Joby watched some more while Gus lifted the mailbags off the pony's back, then he followed Gus and the horse around to the stables. "Gus, you mad at something?"

"No, I ain't mad." He gave the pony a slap that sent it into the stable. Then he turned around. "We had a few troubles. Injuns called on us last night. . . . No, they didn't take nothing, excepting some of my bullets inside their own skins. But they was a bother, keeping Alice and her ma from sleeping. You better eat."

"Station at the Springs had Injun trouble, too," said Joby. "Look, Gus, hadn't I ought to tell Will he should ride now? Huh?"

"Joby," said Gus, "I told you twice already to eat."

Joby went around to the front of the house, sat down on

the doorstep, and took off his boots. The home station that was run by the Webbs was larger and handsomer than any of the other abodes. Mrs. Gus had a real flooring in it, and she and Alice had hung oilcloth at the windows for curtains and muslin from the ceiling to divide the inside off into three separate rooms.

"Gus," Mrs. Webb's voice called, "I want to talk to you!"

"It's me, ma'am," said Joby. "And it's all right; I've took off my boots."

Mrs. Gus came racing out from behind the first lot of curtains, but Joby hardly saw her. Because behind her was Alice.

Alice was prettier even than he had been remembering she was. "Hi," said Joby feebly.

"Hi, Joby," said Alice. She was so pretty and sweet that a man's breath plain got stuck in his windpipe when he was looking at her.

"Hi!" said Joby more loudly.

Mrs. Gus said, "Quiet, Joby. Will is sleeping." She pointed over to the fireplace at a heap of blankets on the floor.

"Will?" said Joby. He tiptoed closer. "Is he sick, ma'am? Or was it the Injuns?"

It was part of one and part of the other, Mrs. Gus said. It was the Indians with their crazy whoopings that had sent Will running to the stables to lock the doors on the horses. But it had been Will's own fancy steppings that had fallen him into the tin tub that was full of doped water for an ailing horse. Mrs. Gus wasn't sure whether Will had got his fever from spending the night in wet clothes or whether it was from the wrench he had given his knee.

After that, for a long time, there wasn't any more talking,

because Alice had brought Joby's food to the table, and it was food that didn't have to be served up with talking. He ate through two helpings of rabbit stew that tasted like chicken, only more tender; then he looked up and grinned at Alice, who was sitting across the table from him, her hands in her lap and her face all over smiles. Then he took off his gun belt and put it on the floor, and then he loosened the belt of his trousers to make some extra room for a third helping of stew. After that there was apple pie to deal with. And he dealt with it joyfully until there wasn't a crumb of the whole pie left on the plate.

"That's pie," said Joby. "It sure is."

"Oh, Joby," said Alice, "it makes me so happy that you're here."

There wasn't any answer a fellow could make to that with words, and until he and Alice were alone, there wasn't any answer he could make to it with kisses. So Joby smiled and Alice smiled, and that made even the apple pie seem unimportant.

"Now, Joby," said Mrs. Gus, "pay attention while I talk to you."

"Yes, ma'am," said Joby politely, and got up, fastening his trousers' belt.

"Joby, Gus has been planning to wait until you're fed and feeling some rested, then he's going to say you should go on with the mail, him being too heavy and Will too sick to ride. But you tell him no, Joby. Tell him maybe to-morrow, if you're feeling fine and the Injuns ain't been seen again, that you'll go. All you've been hired to ride is the miles you've come. There ain't no sense in risking your scalp—"

"Woman," said Gus Webb's voice from the doorway, "I reckon you're forgetting the mail."

Mrs. Gus whirled around. "All the letters in all the sacks in all the world ain't worth one inch of human hair, and you know it, Gus! By morning them devils will be tired of hanging around in the hills, and Joby can make it then. Why, there ain't a soul is going to give a hoot if the mail is one day late."

Gus said, "Long as anybody can carry it, the mail's got to go through." He turned on his heels. "Two minutes, Joby, and there'll be a horse ready for you."

"Please, ma'am," said Joby, "don't you go fretting yourself 'bout Injuns. Them fellows ride ponies so slow you'd think they was going backwards when they're traveling along their fastest. Alice, you tell your ma— Why, Alice—"

"Joby, you can't go now! The Injuns are waiting for you! Joby, you gotta tell Pa you won't go riding no more today! Joby, you hearing me?"

"Aw, Alice, don't you cry. What'd them bucks want with me? Even if they could catch up with me, which they couldn't, why'd they want to try for?"

"Joby," said Mrs. Gus, "you putting a bunch of fool letters ahead of your own girl?"

"Ma'am," said Joby, "somebody's got to carry the mail."

"Joby," said Alice, "if you leave now, I ain't a going to marry you. Not ever I ain't, Joby. You hear me?"

"But, Alice, in two days I'll be back and—"

"If you go now, you don't ever need to come back!"

"But I gotta go, Alice. There ain't nobody else to—"

"All right, you go, and see if I care! I won't care, not one bit I won't care, because I hate you! See? I hate you!"

"Joby!" Gus Webb hollered from the doorway. "Come a running, boy!"

"Alice—" said Joby, but Alice had gone behind the muslin curtain and didn't come out. "Mrs. Gus—" said Joby, but Mrs. Gus had turned her back and was piling up plates on her arm.

"Joby!" Gus Webb hollered again, and Joby went out on the doorstep and sat down and began slowly to pull on his boots. Gus said, "Joby, you paralyzed? Them boots are all right. Come on and get up."

Joby went slowly to where Gus stood rubbing the buckskin's head.

"Now, boy," said Gus, "I ain't saying there's Injuns waiting for you, and I ain't saying there ain't, on account of I don't know. But I'm going to strap a Spencer to your back, just in case. An Injun with a white man's gun is helpless as a rabbit, but with arrows he's poison sure."

A rifle was a heavy thing to carry, but Joby let himself be strapped to it. A rifle wasn't a thing worth arguing about. Nothing was worth arguing about, hardly.

Gus said, "You heard what I been saying, Joby? Straight east to the cut through the mountain. And the canyon brings you out in sight of your first station. You can. . . ."

He turned and Joby turned, too, because the door to the house had been opened.

But it wasn't Alice. It was Mrs. Gus, bringing out the gun belt that Joby had left on the floor.

"Ma'am. . . ." said Joby.

But Mrs. Gus just handed the gun belt to her husband, without even looking at Joby, and went back into the house.

"Women!" said Gus under his breath, and watched while Joby buckled the gun belt low over his hips. Then he handed the reins to Joby and gave the pony a loud slap on the near flank with the flat of his hand. "Good luck!"

Once, before he was out of sight of the house, Joby turned around in his saddle, but the yard was empty and the door to the house was closed.

After that there was nothing to do but ride, so for a long time Joby just rode with his eyes looking straight between the pony's ears at the sand that was ahead of him. There was a queer, hit feeling in Joby's chest, and his throat had got a lump stuck halfway down itself that couldn't right off be swallowed, and together these things took all the strength out of him.

Finally, when he noticed that the pony had slowed down almost to a walk, he shoved his heels back and muttered, "Move along, horse," and got a jerk of speed out of the animal. But the speed didn't last, and after a little the pony was down to a slow lope. Joby let it stay that way, because it took work to keep some horses at a full gallop. And, anyhow, if he did make a record run, the company wouldn't more than say thank you, and all they would think was that next time he should make better speed yet.

All through the years he would have to be riding, making records that nobody would care about. He ached all over now—behind his eyes and between his shoulders and all down his legs—and the sun was so hot that a man and a horse could easily be killed by it. It was a bad country. Tex said it wasn't even fit for cows to get buried in, and that was the truth.

The pony had reached the beginning of the canyon that cut through the mountain, and the going was harder. There was sagebrush and a little greasewood now, and some rocks, and the sand was giving way to a hard roadbed of rock chippings. The pony picked its way with dainty care, once going all of a yard around to sidestep an extra large and prickly greasewood.

Ponies didn't mind having runty-built fellows on their backs. It was girls who wanted men to be big and tall. Mrs. Gus had picked for herself a man that was all of six feet, and that was how a man had to be to make a girl love him.

The pony flattened back its ears, and for a minute Joby thought it was because of the moan he had made without meaning to. But the pony's ears stayed flat, and Joby pushed his hat back from his face and looked up at the sides of the gorge. The sides were still sloping enough for horses and men to have climbed, but there wasn't anything on them that Joby could see, excepting the same old rocks and the sagebrush.

Then he took a quick look behind; and he saw that there were Indians following. There were a lot of them, more than a dozen, but they were back almost at the beginning of the gorge. Joby shoved his heels into the pony's flanks, and when he looked again over his shoulder, his distance from the Indians had already widened. Indians had slow-running, grass-fed ponies, and there never was a time known that they had caught up with a company pony. Ahead there was a turn in the gorge; after the turn his horse would get over its nervousness, too.

Then around the turn ahead came an Indian, and after him three more. Joby pulled hard to the right, and when the pony reared up, he dug both knees into its sides, loosened the reins, and held on. But halfway up the slope, he slithered to a stop and slowly and painfully slid himself off the pony's back. There were three Indians waiting on the ridge above him.

He was stuck all right now. The Indians had been smart. There were three above him and close to twenty spread out below him, and all he could do was wait until they got ready to move into shooting range. Slowly Joby wound the reins around his wrist. Then he unstrapped the rifle from his back and sat down. First the Indians would get him, and while they were getting him, the turkey buzzards would be waiting.

"You want to die?" Joby said fiercely, to get his brain to working, but it didn't help much.

The sun had thickened his head like cotton, and all he could do was sit and watch while the Indians took their positions on the slope, spacing themselves carefully like sentries at Fort Kearney or buzzards on a dead cottonwood. And when they were all spaced and ready, they would charge, and there was nothing that Joby could do to stop them.

He could, maybe, have tried to ride through the weakest point in their circle, but even if he could have managed to shoot a few, he couldn't have outridden the others. Somewhere among them were four who rode on the company ponies that had been stolen from the old man at the Springs. The Indians had been smart, all right, about everything.

Joby turned his head slowly and looked about him. There was no rock near him that was big enough to give him any kind of shelter, and presently he looked again at the pony.

The buckskin had trustful eyes. "Listen, I've gotta have shelter, ain't I?" said Joby aloud. He put his hand to his hip and closed his fingers around his revolver. His hand was tired and discouraged, like his head, and it was hard to get it to care what it did. "Well, ain't I?" Joby said aloud to get speed into himself.

He took a firmer grip of the revolver and pulled. When the gun came out of its holster, it came with a vague, crackling sound, and Joby looked down at it, surprised. The crackling sound had come because a piece of paper had been tied to its barrel.

Joby touched the paper with his fingers, because sometimes in the sun a man, like a horse, will get to seeing mirages. Then he jerked the paper off the gun's barrel and unfolded it.

"Dear Joby," the paper said, "I am still mad at you, but that is because I am afraid you will get hurt. Please be careful of yourself. From your loving Alice."

"Whee!" said Joby. "Ai-yi-yi-eee!"

With a mighty leap he landed squarely in the pony's saddle. Then, with his knees and his heels, he swung the horse around until it faced straight east along the sloping side of the canyon.

Out of the corner of his eye, Joby could see that the bucks down in the valley had wheeled their horses for the chase, and he gave them, shrill and scornful, a coyote's yell.

Then he put his mind on the four Indians that were ahead of him. There was one coming straight on, and another a little up the slope, and two holding the downside. One of the two on the downside carried a rifle and was waving it with both hands. They all four thought that they had him, not knowing how smart he was.

An arrow went by with a whine like a giant bee, and Joby's pony gave a sideways leap and came close to stopping short. Joby pulled sharp to the left, heading the pony straight between the two downhill braves. It was the Indian on his level that had been expecting to meet him, and the others weren't ready for a head-on attack.

"Get aside, you danged idiots!" Joby shouted. The Indian with the rifle, having troubles with his weapon, wheeled, but the other one came straight on, and Joby had to fire. It was Joby's horse that had to jump aside then, because the fellow grabbed at the air like it was a rope to catch hold of and then hit the ground, rolling over twice.

After that the two Indians above him got busy, but Joby had the rider with the rifle between himself and them. Two arrows came close to Joby, one clipping the mane of his pony, but the Indian with the gun, riding neck to neck with him, made a fine shelter.

It was a company pony that the Indian was on, and that was his bad luck, because he and Joby had outraced the other two, and they were both so close together that neither he nor Joby could get hold of a chance to fire.

Then, suddenly, the Indian got some sort of idea, because Joby saw him raise himself way up in his saddle. But Joby got an idea too; and he worked his out quicker. He gave a howl and threw Gus Webb's Spencer, butt end, to his right.

It must have hit the Indian in a tender place, because after that Joby rode alone up in front.

He rode, leaning forward on his horse's neck, and all the buckskin had to do was run. It did that even better than an antelope could, because an antelope has to run riderless, and the buckskin had a smart fellow on its back.

Chances were the mail wouldn't even be late now. Chances were he would make another record with it. Alice would like that, two records in one day.

"Yi-yi-yi-eee!" Joby howled again, because of the fun he was having.

CALL THIS LAND HOME

ERNEST HAYCOX

One at a time, the emigrant families fell out where the
land most pleased them, and at last only two wagons of the
overland caravan moved southward along the great green
valley of Oregon; then the Potters discovered their fair
place and John Mercy drove on with his lone wagon, his
wife in unhappy silence beside him, and Caroline and
young Tom under the canvas cover behind. Through the
puckered opening at the wagon's rear young Tom saw the

Potters grow dim in the steaming haze of this wet day.
Rain lightly drummed on the canvas as he listened to the
talk of his people.

"Have we got to live so far from everybody?" his mother
asked.

In his father's voice was that fixed mildness which young
Tom knew so well. "The heart of a valley's always better
than foot or head. I want two things—the falls of a creek for
my mill and plenty of open land roundabout."

She said, "Rough riding won't do for me much longer."

"I know," he said, and drove on.

In middle afternoon two days later the wagon stopped,
and his father said, "I believe we're here." Crawling over
the tail gate, young Tom—Thomas Jackson Mercy, age
eight—saw the place on which he was to spend the rest of
his long life. In three directions the fall-cast green earth ran
off in the gentle meadow vistas, here and there interrupted
by low knobs and little islands of timber, and crosshatched
by the brushy willow borders of creeks. On the fourth side
a hill covered by fir and cedar ran down upon the wagon.
A stream smaller than a river, but bigger than a branch,
came across the meadows, dropped over a two-foot rock
ledge like a bent sheet of glittering glass, and sharply
curved to avoid the foot of the hill, running on toward some
larger stream beyond view.

John Mercy turned toward the wagon to give his wife
a hand, and young Tom noted that she came down with a
careful awkwardness. Then his father stamped the spongy
earth with his feet and bent over and plunged his tough
fingers into the soil and brought up a sample, squeezing
and crumbling it, and considering it closely. He was a very
tall man, a very powerful man, and all his motions were

governed by a willful regularity. A short curly beard covered his face as far as the cheekbones; a big nose, scarred white at the bridge, stood over a mouth held firm by constant habit. He seemed to be smiling, but it was less a smile than a moment of keen interest that forced little creases around mouth and eyes. To young Tom, his father, at twenty-eight, was an old man.

John Mercy said, "It will take a week of clear weather to dry this ground for plowing." He turned, looking at the timber close by, and at the rising slope of the hill; he put his hands on his hips, and young Tom knew his father was searching out a place for the cabin. A moment later Mercy swung to face his wife with a slightly changed expression. She had not moved since leaving the wagon; she stood round-shouldered and dejected in the soft rain, reflecting on her face the effect of the gray day, the dampness and the emptiness that lay all around them. Young Tom had never seen her so long idle, for she was brisk in everything she did, always moving from chore to chore.

Mercy said, "In another two years you'll see neighbors wherever you look."

"That's not now," she said.

"The Willamette's beyond this hill somewhere. There's settlers on it."

She said, "I long for back home," and turned from him and stood still again, facing the blind distance.

John Mercy stepped to the wagon and lifted the ax from its bracket. He said to young Tom, "Go cut a small saplin' for a pole, and some uprights," and handed over the ax. Then he got into the wagon and swung it around to drive it under the trees. When young Tom came out of the deeper timber with his saplings, the oxen were unyoked and a fire burned beneath the massive spread of a cedar. The tail gate was down, and his father had reversed an empty tub to make a step from wagon to ground. Between them, they made a frame for the extra tarpaulin to rest on, thereby creating a shelter. His mother stood by, still with her unusual helplessness on her, and he knew, from his father's silence, that there was trouble between them.

His father said, "Water, Tom," and went on working. When Tom came back with the big camp kettle filled, his father had driven uprights at either side of the fire, connected by a crosspiece on which the hook hung. He lifted the camp kettle to the hook and listened a moment to the fire hissing against the kettle's wet bottom. The grub box was let down from the wagon box, and his mother was idle at the fire, one arm around Caroline, who stood by her. His father was at the edge of the timber, facing the meadow; he went over.

"Now, then," his father said, "It's sickly weather and we've got to get up a cabin. It'll go here. We'll cut the small trees yonder, for that's where the good house will stand someday. So we'll be doing two things at the same time— making the cabin and clearing the yard." His eyes, gray to their bottommost depths, swung around, and their effect was like heavy weight on young Tom. It was seldom that he gave young Tom this undivided attention. "We've got everything to do here, and nothing to do it with but our hands. Never waste a lick, and make every lick work twice for you if you can. No man lives long enough to get done all he wants to do, but if he works slipshod and has got to do it over, then he wastes his life. I'll start on that tree. You trim and cut."

The blows of the ax went through the woods in dull echo-

ing, not hurried—for his father never hurried—but with
the even tempo of a clock's ticking. His mother worked
around the grub box with her disheartened slowness. First
shadows were sooty in the timber and mist moved in from
the meadows. He listened to the sounds of the empty land
with tight fascination; he watched the corridors of the timber for moving things, and he waited for the tree to fall.

The rains quit. Warmed by a mild winter sun, the
meadows exhaled fleecy wisps of steam, which in young
Tom's imagination became the smoke of underground fires
breaking through. They dropped trees of matched size, cut
and notched and fitted them. When the walls were waist
high, Mercy rigged an incline and a block and tackle, but
even with that aid his body took the weight of each log,
his boots sank deep into the spongy soil and his teeth
showed in white flashes when hard effort pulled back his
lips.

After supper, with a fire blazing by the cabin, he adzed
out the rough boards for window and doorframes and inner
furniture, and late at night young Tom woke to hear his
father's froe and mallet splitting the cedar roof shakes, and
sometimes heard his mother fretfully calling. "Mercy, come
now! It's late enough!" Lying awake, he listened to his
father come into the wagon and settle down upon the mat-
tress with a groaning sigh and fall at once asleep. The dying
yellow of the firelight flickered against the wagon canvas;
strange sounds rustled in the windy woods, and far off was
the baying of timber wolves. Caroline, disturbed by that
wild sound, stirred against him.

The rains held off and the meadows dried before the
roof of the cabin was on. John Mercy said, "It might be the

last clear spell all winter. I have got to stop the cabin and break that meadow and get the wheat in." He looked at his wife. "Maybe you won't mind living in the wagon a week longer."

"I mind nothing," she said, "except being here."

John Mercy turned to his son. "Go round up the animals."

The two brindle oxen were deep in the meadow. Driving them back to the cabin, young Tom saw his people at the campfire; they were saying things not meant for him, his mother with her arms tight across her breasts and her head flung up. Presently his father turned away to yoke the oxen, hitch on the breaking plow, and go into the meadow.

The ancient turf became coiled, gloss-brown strips. John Mercy watched the sky as he plowed, and plowed until the furrows grew ragged in the fading day; and ate and built his fire and hewed out the cabin rafters, and by morning's first twilight shadows he was at work again, harrowing the meadow into its rough clods, into its pebbled smoothness. The gray clouds thickened in the southwest and the wind broke and whirled them on. With the wheat sack strapped before him like an apron, John Mercy sowed his grain, reaching for the seed, casting with an even sweep, pacing on, and reaching and casting again. Young Tom sawed out the top logs, shortening and angling each cut meant for the cabin's peak; and at night, by the bonfire's swaying glow, he laid his weight against the block-and-tackle rope while his father heaved the logs up the incline into place.

On Sunday his father said, "Take the gun, Tom, and go over this hill and keep on till you find the Willamette. See what you can see. Come back around the side of the hill and tell me which is the short way."

Within a hundred yards the cabin vanished behind the great bark-ribbed trunks of firs whose trunks were thicker through than the new cabin. They ran far to the sky and an easy cry came out of them as they swayed to the wind. Pearly shafts of light slanted down into this still wilderness place, like the shafts of judgment light shining from heaven to earth in Redway's old geography book. Fern and hazel stood head high to him, and giant deadfalls lay with their red-brown rotted wood crumbling away.

He climbed steadily, now and then crossing short ravines in whose black marsh bottom the devil stock stiffly grew, and stung him as he passed; and down a long vista he saw a buck deer poised alertly at a pool. His gun rose, but then he heard the cool advice of his father, "Never shoot meat far from home," and he slapped his hand against the gun stalk and watched the deer go bounding into the deeper forest gloom.

A long two miles brought him to the crest of the hill, from which he saw the surface of a big river in smooth patches between the lower trees. Another half mile, very rough, brought him down to the river's margin; he turned to the right and presently the timber and the hill rolled out into the meadowlands. Directly over the river he saw a cabin in a clearing, and saw a girl at the break of the bluff, watching him. He looked at her and suffered his short shock of disappointment to find a house and people here, for he had been until this moment a lone explorer pushing through a wild and empty place.

At such a distance he could not clearly see her face; she was about his size, and she stared at him with a motionless interest. He stirred his feet in the soft earth and he raised his hand and waved it, but she continued to look at him, not answering, and in a little while he turned and followed the open meadows as they bent around the toe of the dark hill and reached home before noon.

His father said, "What did you see?"

"The river's on the other side of the hill, but it's easier to go around the hill. I saw a deer."

"That's all?"

"And a cabin across the river," said Tom. "There was a girl in the yard."

John Mercy looked at his wife. "Now," he said quietly, "there's one neighbor," and waited for her answer.

She looked at him, reluctant to be pleased. "How far away?"

Young Tom said, "More than an hour, I guess."

His mother said, "If they saw you, they'll come to visit . . . and it's a terrible camp they'll see. . . . Caroline, go scrub and change your dress. I've got to fix your hair." Suddenly she was irritably energetic, moving around to put away the scattered pans and the loose things lying under the canvas shelter.

John Mercy went toward a pile of saplings roughly cut into rafters; he cast a secret glance of benevolence at young Tom. Something had pleased him. He said, "We'll get these on in short order."

The saplings went up and crosspoles were set across them. The first row of shakes was laid when a man's strong halloo came ringing in from the meadow and a family moved through the trees, man and wife, two tall boys carrying sacks, and the girl young Tom had noticed across the river.

The man said in a great, grumbling voice, "Neighbor, by the Lord, we could of saved you sweat on that cabin if we'd known you were here. Teal's my name. Iowa."

Talk broke through this quiet like a sudden storm. The two women moved beyond the wagon, and young Tom heard their voices rush back and forth in tumbling eagerness. The men were at the cabin.

Teal said, "Boys, you're idle. This man needs shakes for his roof. Go split 'em. . . . It's a going to rain, Mercy, and when it rains here, it's the world drowned out. The drops are big as banty eggs. They bust like ripe watermelons, they splatter, they splash. You're soaked, your shoes squash, you steam like a kettle on fire. . . . Boys, don't stand there. Mercy and me will lay on what shakes that's cut."

The Teal girl stood in front of young Tom and stared at him with direct curiosity. She was not quite his height; she was berry brown, with small freckles on her nose, and her hair hung down behind in one single braid. Caroline cautiously moved forward and looked up to the Teal girl, and suddenly put out a hand and touched her dress. The Teal girl took Caroline's hand, but she kept her eyes on young Tom.

"I saw you," she said.

"What's your name?"

"Mary," said the Teal girl, and turned with the quickest motion and walked toward the older women.

The Teal boys worked on shakes, one splitting, one drawing the cedar panels down with the knife. The wind lifted and the roar of it was the dashing of giant cataracts all through the deep places of the forest; the men talked steadily as they worked. The smell of frying steak—brought by the Teals—was in the air to tantalize young Tom. He leaned against a tree and watched Mary Teal from the corner of his eye, then turned and walked away from the trees to the falls of the creek and squatted at the edge of the pool, his shadow sending the loafing trout into violent crisscross flight. Gray clouds ran low over the land and a deepening haze crawled forward. He hunched himself together, like a savage over a fire; he listened into the wind and waited for the scurrying shapes of the enemy to come trotting in war file out of the misty willow clumps. He sat there a long while, the day growing dull around him. The wind increased and the pool's silver surface showed the pocking of rain. His mother's voice called him back to mealtime.

He ate by the fire, listening to the voices of the older people go on and on. His mother's face was red from the heat of the fire, and her eyes were bright, and she was smiling; his father sat comfortably under the cedar tree, thawed by the company. It was suddenly half-dark, the rain increasing, and the Teals rose and spoke their farewells and filed off through the trees, Mr. Teal's last cheerful call returning to them. Silence returned; loneliness deepened.

His mother said, "It was good to see people."

"They'll be fine neighbors," his father said.

His mother's face tightened. She looked over the flames and suddenly seemed to remember her fears. "Four miles away," she said, and turned to the dishes on the camp table. She grew brisk. "Tom, I want water. . . . Stack these dishes, Caroline, and come out of the rain."

John Mercy went into the darkness beyond the cabin and built his work fire; lying awake in bed, young Tom heard his father's mallet steadily splitting out shakes, and he continued to hear the sound in his sleep.

By morning a great wind cried across the world. John
Mercy lighted the campfire and cooked breakfast for the
women within the wagon. He laid on heavy logs for the
fire's long burning and took up a piece of rope and the ax
and hammer and nails. "We have got a chore to do at the
river," he said to young Tom. "You pack the gun." They
skirted the foot of the hill, trailing beside a creek stained
muddy by the underfoot, and the southwest wind roughly
shoved them forward through sheets of fat raindrops spark-
ling in the mealy light. When they reached the river they
saw a lamp burning in the window of the Teal house, but
John Mercy swung to a place where the hill's timber met
the bluff of the stream.

"There will come a time," he said, "when I'll have to send
you to the Teals' for help. You'll need a raft to cross."

They cut down and trimmed six saplings for a raft bed,
bound them with two crosspieces nailed in. A pole, chipped
flat at one end, made an oar. Then John Mercy tied the
rope to the raft and towed it upstream a hundred yards beyond the Teal house. He drew it half from the water and
secured the rope to an overhanging tree, and laid the oar
in the brush. "You'll drift as you paddle," he said.

Homeward-bound, the wind came at them face on.
Young Tom bent against it, hearing his father's half-shouted
words, "It ought to be a month or more before the baby's
due. But we're alone out here, and accidents come along.
We've got to expect those things. No sensible man watches
his feet hit ground. He looks ahead to see what kind of
ground they'll hit next."

They came around a bend of the creek and heard a massive cannon crack of sound in the hills above them, and the
ripping fall of a tree; its jarring collision with the earth ran

out to them. They pressed on, John Mercy's pace quicken-
ing as though a new thought disturbed him. High in the
air was an echo like the crying of a bird, lasting only a moment and afterward shredded apart by the storm, but it
rose again, thinner and wilder, and became a woman's voice
screaming.

John Mercy's body broke from its channeled steadiness
and he rushed around the last bend of the hill, past the pool
of the falls, and into the cabin clearing. Young Tom followed, the gun across his chest. Through the trees he saw
a figure by the campfire, not his mother's figure, but a dark
head and a dark face standing above some kind of cloak.
His father stopped at the fire before the stranger; reaching
the scene, young Tom discovered that the stranger was an
Indian. His mother stood back against the wagon with a
butcher knife in her hand; her face shocked him, white and
strange-stretched as it was.

He lifted the gun, waiting. The Indian was old and his
cheeks were round holes rimmed by jawbone and temple.
His eyes were sick. His hand, stretched through the blanket,
was like the foot of a bird, nothing but bone and wrinkled
dark flesh. He spoke something, he pointed at the food
locker. For a moment—for a time-stopped space in which
the acid clarity of this scene ate its way so deeply into
young Tom's memory that ninety years of living neither
changed nor dimmed a detail of it—he watched the latent
danger rise around his father's mouth and flash his eyes;
then, with complete unexpectedness, his father turned to
the grub box and found half a loaf of bread. His father
pointed at the gun in young Tom's hand and pointed back
to the Indian, snapping down his thumb as though firing; he
seized the Indian at the hips, lifting him like a half-emptied

sack, walked a few steps and dropped him and gave an onward push. The Indian went away without looking behind him, his shoulders bent.

His mother's voice, high-pitched and breathless, drew young Tom's attention. She was shaking, and in her eyes was a great wildness. "I don't want to be here! I didn't want to come! Mercy, you've got to take me home! I want my old house back! I want my people! I'll die here!"

John Mercy said, "Tom, take your sister for a walk."

Caroline stood in the doorway of the cabin, frightened by the scene. Young Tom went over to catch her hand. The half-covered roof kept Caroline dry, and he stood indecisively under this shelter disliking to leave it, yet compelled by his father's order.

John Mercy lifted his wife into his arms, speaking, "The creature was harmless. There are no bad Indians around here. I know the weather's poor and there's no comfort, but I'll have the roof on the cabin by tonight." He carried her into the wagon, still talking.

Young Tom heard his mother's voice rising again, and his father's patient answering. He clung to Caroline's hand and watched the rainswept world beyond the cabin and saw no other shelter to which he might go. He was hard pressed to make up his mind, and when his father came out of the wagon, he said in self-defense, "Caroline would get awfully wet if I took her for a walk."

John Mercy said, "You did right. . . . Caroline, go keep your mother company." He looked up to the unfinished roof, he drew a hand down across his water-crusted beard, and for a moment he remained stone-still, his whole body sagged down with its accumulation of weariness. He drew a long breath and straightened. "Soon as I finish the roof,

Tom, we'll line the fireplace with clay. I'll need some straw to mix with the clay. You go along the creek where the old hay's rotted down. Bring me several swatches of it."

The rain walked over the earth in constant sheets, beating down grass and weeds and running vines; the creek grew violent between its banks and the increased falls dropped roaring into its pool. Bearing his loads of dead grass to the cabin, young Tom watched his father lay the last rows of shakes on the roof and cap the ridge with boards hewn out earlier, by the late firelight; afterward John Mercy, working faster against the fading day, went beside the creek to an undercut bank and shoveled out its clay soil, carrying it back to the cabin by bucket. He cooked a quick supper and returned to the cabin, mixing clay and dead-grass stems, and coated the wood fireplace and its chimney with this mortar. He built a small fire, which, by drying the mud, would slowly season it to a brick-hard lining.

Throughout the night, fitfully waking, young Tom heard the dull thumping of a hammer, and twice heard his mother call out, "Mercy, come to bed!" At daybreak young Tom found a canvas door at the cabin; inside, a fire burned on the dirt hearth and a kettle steamed from the crane. The crevices between logs were mud-sealed, the table and grub box and benches had been brought in. Standing before the fire, young Tom heard the wind search the outer wall and fall away, and suddenly the warmth of the place thawed the coldness which lay beneath his skin. He heard his mother come in, and he turned to see his parents standing face to face, almost like strangers.

His mother said, "Mercy, did you sleep at all?"

His father's answer was somehow embarrassed. "I had

to keep the fire alive, so the mud would dry right. Today I'll get the puncheons on the floor and we can move the beds in." In a still gentler voice, the uncertainess of apology in it, his father added, "Maybe, if you shut your eyes and think how all this will look five years from now—"

She cut him off with the curt swing of her body, and walked to the fire. Stooping with a slowness so unlike her, she laid the Dutch oven against the flame and went to the grub box. She put her yellow mixing bowl on the table, she got her flour and her shortening and her salt. She stood a moment over the mixing bowl, not looking at John Mercy. "As long as I can do my share, I'll do it . . . . Tom, fetch me the pail of water."

He stood with his father at the break of the trees, viewing the yellow-gray ground beyond it, and the valley floor running away to the great condensed wall of mist. He knew, from the dead gentleness of tone, that his father was very tired; it was not like him to waste time speaking of the future. "The orchard will go right in front of this spot," his father said. "That will be pretty to look at from the house. The house will stand where we're standing. These firs will go down." He was silent, drawing the future forward and finding comfort in it. "All this is free—all this land. But it's up to a man to make something out of it. So there's nothing free. There never is. We'll earn every acre we get. Don't trust that word *free*. Don't believe it. You'll never own anything you didn't pay for. But what you pay for is yours. You've got it while other men wait around for something free, and die with nothing. Now, then, we have to cut down some small firs, about eight inches through. We'll split them in half for floor puncheons."

He turned, walking slower than usual; he searched the

trees, nodding at one or the other, and stopped at a thin fir starved by the greater firs around it; its trunk ran twenty feet without a branch. "That one," he said, and went to the cabin wall for his ax. "Tom," he said, "I want you to go up in the hills and see how close you can find a ledge of rock. That's for the fireplace floor." He faced the tree, watching the wind whip its top; he made an undercut on the side toward which he wished the tree to fall, and squared himself away to a steady chopping.

Young Tom passed the cabin, upward bound into the semidarkness of the hill; the great trees groaned in their swaying, and their shaken branches let down ropy spirals of rain. It was like walking into a tunnel full of sound. His overcoat grew heavy with water, which, dripping on his trousers' legs, turned them into ice-cold bands; his shoes were mushy. Behind him he heard the first crackling of the tree going down, and he turned and saw his father running. The tree, caught by the wind, was falling the wrong way. He shouted against the wind; his father looked behind, saw the danger, and jumped aside. The tree, striking a larger fir, bounced off, and young Tom saw its top branches whip out and strike his father to the ground. His father shouted, buried somewhere beneath that green covering.

His mother came crying out of the cabin. "Mercy! Mercy!" She stumbled and caught herself, and rushed on, fighting the branches away as she reached the tree.

When he got there, he saw his father lying with both legs beneath the trunk. The branches, first striking, had broken the force of the trunk's fall; and then they had shattered, to let the trunk down upon his father, who lay on an elbow with his lips the color of gray flour paste. Young

Tom never knew until then how piercing a gray his father's
eyes were.

His mother cried, "Your legs! Oh, God, Mercy!" She
bent over him, she seized the trunk of the tree and she
stiffened under her straining. John Mercy's voice was a
vast shout of warning, "Nancy, don't do that!" His arms
reached out and struck her on the hip. "Let go!" She drew
back and laid both arms over her stomach, a shock of pain
pressing her face into its sharp angles. "Oh, Mercy," she
said, "it's too late!" and stared down at him in terror.

Young Tom raced to the cabin wall, got the shovel, and
rushed back; a branch interfered with his digging. He
found the ax, thrown ten yards away by Mercy in his flight;
he returned to cut the limb away. Mercy lay still, as though
he were listening. He watched his wife, and he put a hand
over his eyes and seemed to be thinking; the impact of the
ax on the trunk threw twinges of pain through him, but he
said nothing until young Tom had finished.

"Give me the shovel," he said. "Now go get Mrs. Teal."

Young Tom stood irresolute. "You got to get out of there."

"Those legs," said John Mercy, and spoke of them as
though they didn't belong to him, "are pinched. If they
were broken, I'd know it . . . and they're not." He paused
and a dead gray curtain of pain came down on his face; he
suffered it and waited for it to pass. "Do as I tell you."
Young Tom whirled and started away at a hard run, and
was almost instantly checked and swung by his father's
command. "You've got a long way to go, and you'll not do
it starting that fast. Steady now. I've told you before . . .
think ahead."

Young Tom began again, trotting out upon the meadow;
he looked back and saw his father awkwardly working with

the shovel, sheltered by the outstretched apron of his mother. But even before young Tom ceased to look, she dropped the apron, put both hands before her face and walked toward the wagon.

The scene frightened him, and he broke into a dead run along the margin of the creek, and began to draw deep into his lungs for wind; he ran with his fists doubled, his arms lunging back and forth across his chest. A pain caught him in the side, and he remembered his father's advice and slowed to a dogtrot. He grew hot and stopped once to crawl down the bank of a creek for a drink, and was soon chilled by the wet ground against his stomach and the rain beating on his back.

After a rest of a minute he went on, stiffened by that short pause. The river willows at last broke through the rain mist forward, and the low shape of the Teal cabin. He crossed the last meadow and came to the bank; he hadn't forgotten the raft, but he wanted to save time. The wind was with him, carrying his shrill call over the water. He repeated it twice before the cabin door opened and Mrs. Teal stepped to the yard. Young Tom raised his arm, pointing behind him toward his home. Mrs. Teal waved back at him immediately and ran into the house.

Squatted on the bank, young Tom saw the three Teal men come out, lift a boat and carry it to the water; in a moment Mrs. Teal joined them, and the four came over the river. Mrs. Teal had a covered basket in her hand. She said, "Your mother, Tom?"

"My father's caught under a sapling that fell on him. That made mother sick."

Teal turned on his lank, Indian-dark sons. "Git ahead and help him."

"Oh, Lord, Lord," said Mrs. Teal. "Take the basket, Nate. We've got to go fast. It's going to be unnatural."

Young Tom started after the Teal boys, they running away with a loose and ranging ease. "No," said Teal, "you stay with us. You've had runnin' enough. The boys are a pair of hounds; let 'em go."

They went forward, Mrs. Teal now and then speaking to herself with a soft exclamation of impatience. Otherwise there was no talk. The wind was against them and the rain beat down. Young Tom opened his mouth to let the great drops loosen his dry throat, and silently suffered the slow pace. The coming baby never entered his mind; it was of his father lying under the tree that he thought with dread, and when the creek began to bend around the toe of the hills, close by the falls, he ran ahead and reached the house.

His father had dug himself out from the trap; there was a little tunnel of earth where he had been. The two boys stood silently at the fire, and one of them motioned toward the cabin. Young Tom drew the doorway canvas back from the logs, looking in: his father had moved the bedstead from the wagon and had set it up near the cabin's fireplace. His mother was on it, groaning, and his father knelt at the bedside and held her hands. Young Tom retreated to the fire, watching the Teals come through the trees. Mrs. Teal seized the basket from her husband and went at once into the cabin; a moment later his father came out.

John Mercy said to Teal, "It's a good thing to have neighbors. I'm sorry I can't offer you coffee at this minute." He let his chin drop and he spread his hands before the fire and gravely watched it. The sockets of his eyes seemed deep and blackened; his mouth was a line straight and narrow across his skin.

"My friend," said Teal, "the first winter's always a bad one. Don't work so hard or you'll be twenty years older by spring." He turned to the taller of his two sons. "Jack, take Mercy's gun and go fetch in a deer."

Young Tom heard his mother's sharp cry from the cabin. He moved away, he stood by the tree and stared at the trench in which his father had been, and noticed the marks scrubbed into the soft ground by his father's elbows. He walked along the tree and gave it a kick with his foot, and continued to the millpond. There he squatted, watching the steamy mists pack tighter along the willows of the creek. In the distance, a mile or so, a little timbered butte stood half-concealed by the fog, seeming to ride free in the low sky. He tightened his muscles, waiting for the enemy to come single file through the brush, but then he thought of the old savage, so bony and stooped and unclean, who had seized the half loaf of bread, and his picture of a row of glistening copper giants was destroyed. He heard voices by the cabin, and rose and saw Mrs. Teal by the fire. He went back.

Mrs. Teal looked at him with her kindness. "Your mother's all right, Tom. You had a brother, but he wasn't meant to stay. You understand, Tom? It's meant that way and you oughtn't sorrow."

She meant the baby boy was dead. He thought about it and waited to feel like crying, but he hadn't seen this boy and he didn't know anything about him, and didn't know what to cry for. It embarrassed him not to feel sad. He stood with his eyes on the fire.

Teal said to his other son, "That Methodist preacher is probably down at Mission Bottom, Pete. You go home, get the horse, and go for him." He walked a little distance onward, speaking in a lower tone to his son. Then the son went on, and Teal turned back to the cabin and got the saw standing by the wall and went over to the fallen log. He called to young Tom, "Now then, let's not be idle, man. Puncheons he wanted, wasn't it? We'll just get 'em ready while we wait."

A shot sounded deeper in the forest—one and no more. "There's your meat," said Teal. "You've seen the trout in the creek, ain't you? Mighty fat. Next summer there'll be quail all through those meadow thickets. What you've got to have is a horse for ridin'. Just a plain ten-dollar horse. I know where there's one."

The minister arrived around noon the next day, and out of this wet and empty land the neighbors began to come, riding or walking in from all quarters of the mist-hidden valley, destroying forever young Tom's illusion of wilderness. They came from the scattered claims along the river, from French Prairie, from the upper part of the La Creole, from the strangely named creeks and valleys as far as twenty miles away; the yard was filled with men, and women worked in the cabin and at the fire outside the cabin. Young Tom stared at strange boys running through the timber, and resented their trespassing; he heard girls giggling in the shelter of the wagon. It was a big meeting. A heavy man in buckskins, light of eye and powerfully voiced, strolled through the crowd and had a word for everyone. People visited and the talk was of the days of the wagon-train crossing, of land here and land there, of politics and the Hudson's Bay Company. A group of men walked along the break of the hill until they reached a knoll a hundred yards from the cabin. He watched them digging.

In a little while they returned, bringing quietness to the people. The minister came from the cabin, bareheaded in the rain. Mr. Teal followed, carrying a small bundle wrapped within a sheet and covered by a shawl; they went on toward the grave, and young Tom, every sense sharpened, heard the knocking of a hammer and the calling of a voice. The crowd moved over and his father walked from the cabin, carrying his mother. Young Tom saw Caroline alone at the cabin's doorway, crying; he went to her and got her hand and followed his father.

A little box stood at the grave, the minister by it; he had a book in his hand, which he watched while the rain dripped down his long face. Young Tom's mother was on her feet, but she wasn't crying, though all the women around her were. The minister spoke a long while, it seemed to Tom. He held Caroline's hand and grew cold, waiting for the minister's words to end. Somebody said, "Amen," and the minister began a song, all the people joining.

Looking at his feet, young Tom felt the coldness run up his legs, and his chest was heavy and he, too, cried. As soon as the song was done, his father carried his mother back to the house, and the crowd returned to the fire. A woman dumped venison steaks into a big kettle on the table, and cups and plates went around and the talk grew brisker than it had been before.

Young Tom said, "Caroline, you go into the wagon." From the corners of his eyes he saw men shoveling dirt into the grave; he thought about the grave and imagined the rains filling it with water, and the shawl and the white sheet growing black in the mud. He went over to the fallen log and sat on it.

He remained there, wholly lost in the forest of his imagination while the roundabout neighbors, finished with eating and finished with visiting, started homeward through the dulling day. They went in scattered groups, as they had come, their strong calling running back and forth in the windy rain; and at last only the Teals remained. He saw Caroline and Mary Teal watching him through the front opening of the wagon. He rose and went around to the cabin, hearing the older Teals talking.

Mrs. Teal said, "I'm needed. We'll stay tonight."

Teal looked at his two tall sons. "You had best get at those puncheons. Mercy's legs will trouble him for a while. Tomorrow we are a goin' to knock down some trees for a barn lean-to."

Young Tom quietly drew back the canvas covering of the cabin's doorway. He was troubled about his mother and wanted to see her, and meant to go in. But what he saw suddenly shut him out and brought great embarrassment to him.

His father stood beside the bed, looking down, and young Tom heard him say, "I can't stay here when your heart's not in it. There is no pleasure in this work, and no point in looking ahead to what it'll be someday, if you don't feel it too. Well, you don't. We'll go home . . . in the spring when it's possible to travel. That's what you want, I clearly know."

She was pale and her eyes were stretched perfectly round; her head rolled slightly, her voice was very small. "I couldn't leave now. I've got a baby buried here. It's a mighty hard way to come to love a country . . . to lose

something in it. Mercy, put a railing around that grave. I
have not been of much use, I know, and it's hurt me to see
you work the way you've done. It will be better when I can
get up and do what I can do."

John Mercy bent down and kissed his wife, and suddenly
in young Tom the embarrassment became intolerable, for
this was a thing he had never seen his people do before,
and a thing he was to see again only twice so long as they
lived. He pulled back and let the canvas fall into place; he
thought he heard his father crying. He walked by the big
kettle with its remaining chunks of fried venison steak. He
took one, eating it like a piece of bread. Caroline and Mary
Teal were now at the back end of the wagon, looking at
him.

He said, "I know a big cave up on the hill."

Mary Teal came from the wagon, Caroline following;
and the three walked into the woods, into the great sea
swells of sound poured out by the rolling timber crowns.
Mary gave him a sharp sidewise glance and smiled, destroying the strangeness between them and giving him a
mighty feeling of comfort. The long, long years were beginning for Tom Mercy, and he was to see that smile so
many times again in the course of his life, to be warmed
and drawn on by it, to see tears shining through it, and
broken thoughts hidden by it. To the last day of his life
far out in another century, that smile—real or long after
remembered—was his star, but like a star, there was a
greater heat within it than he was ever to feel or to know.